HEAVEN ON EARTH

COMPASS BOYS, BOOK 1

JAYNE RYLON

MARI CARR

HAPPY ENDINGS PUBLISHING

Cover Art By Jayne Rylon

Version 4

eBook ISBN: 978-1-941785-82-9

Print ISBN: 978-1-941785-83-6

Compass Boys, Book 1

A brand new, never before released standalone story in the Compass saga from New York Times and USA Today bestselling authors Jayne Rylon and Mari Carr.

Austin Compton has struggled to live up to the Compass legacy his entire life, afraid of disappointing his overachieving family. After dropping out of college, he convinced his parents to buy a big rig and let him contribute to the Compass Ranch in his own way.

On the open road he discovers a happy medium between the freedom he craves and the obligation that comes along with the Compton name. When he picks up some unexpected cargo in the form of a gorgeous if battered stowaway, he's in trouble. The same reckless urges that convinced him to abandon his education are telling him to keep Hayden close and safe, maybe even teach her how to love again after the disastrous relationship she's fleeing.

When troubled times fall on Compass Ranch, Hayden will do anything to repay the kindness Austin and his family showed her. It's time to support Austin like he's done for her, if her past doesn't catch up with her at exactly the wrong moment.

PROLOGUE

"What the hell are you doing here, kid?" Jake shouted from the opposite side of the ridge overlooking Compass Ranch. The kickass cowboy galloped over fast enough to give those prissy thoroughbreds in the Kentucky Derby a run for their money, making Austin Compton nearly drop dead of a heart attack.

Damn it! There was no hiding now. He'd been busted. Big time.

"Uh. Would you believe I'm working on some kind of independent study about ranching?" Austin scuffed his boot in the dirt outside the tent he'd been squatting in for nearly a week.

"For a fancy technology something-or-other major? Don't give me no bullshit." Jake swung his leg over his enormous draft horse and dropped to the ground. He was awfully spry for a man who'd turned sixty-five last year and had labored hard on the ranch for more than four decades. Hell, the guy had originally worked for Austin's grandfather, the infamous JD Compton. Though Austin had never met his true blood ancestor, who'd died of cancer before he'd been born, Jake had been a fixture in his life. As much a part of his home as this place and the rest of the family who lived here.

God, he'd missed them so much.

Would they be even a little happy to see him? Or would his colossal failure make him less worthy of a place here with them? The sickness swirling through his gut made it impossible to speak. He clutched his middle.

Jake didn't relent. "Well? A line as lame as that ain't gonna fly with me and it certainly isn't going to fool your dads. So you might as well use this as a test run and fill me in before you have to face them. Maybe I can help you out of whatever mess you've gotten yourself into this time."

Austin groaned and dropped to the ground. He tried to make it seem like he'd flopped there on purpose instead of at the mercy of his wobbly knees. Dread over this exact scenario had kept him at college for two years despite the fact he'd known he wasn't cut out for academia by the time he'd finished moving into the dorm and realized there was nowhere to hang his cowboy hat. He couldn't even open the windows of his shoebox room on the twelfth floor of the damn building.

How could someone live without fresh air?

"I couldn't do it. I'm a fucking quitter," he blurted. "I dropped out."

"Of school?" Jake took his hat off and slapped it against his palm, launching a cloud of dust into the air.

Austin nodded.

"Oh boy." Jake sank into a squat beside him, studying the earth beneath their boots.

"Exactly." He hung his head, crushing his skull between his hands. What was he going to do now?

"Were your grades shit?"

"Nah. I had one C. Mostly B's and a few A's."

"Then what's the problem, kid?"

"I didn't belong there. My roommate came back from class

one day shouting that we were almost halfway to finishing our degrees. He was dancing on top of his crappy desk, knocking more shit on the floor, and planning on getting shit-faced to celebrate. Meanwhile, I felt sick. There was absolutely no way I could hang in that long. Every minute I spent there was torture. And for what? A career I'd hate just as much?" Austin ripped a weed out of the ground as he took in the landscape before him.

He forced himself to take a deep breath. Then another.

From the crest overlooking his family's ranchland, he studied the cows dotting the pastures below. In the distance, the farmhouse, barns, and the row of cottages his sisters lived in were barely visible. Snow-capped mountains spiked into the air around them. A wide river snaked through the long grass.

He held the crisp Wyoming air in his lungs, then slowly began to relax.

It was familiar. Home. Perfect.

Jake nodded. "I never did get how your Uncle Sam survived in New York City so long before coming back home. I sure couldn't live like that."

"There were people everywhere, one on top of another. Everyone rushed around all the time and weren't connected to the things surrounding them. The other students could hardly understand my accent and...well, it just wasn't me." Austin sighed.

"Maybe Phoenix wasn't the right choice. Since you didn't flunk, you could transfer someplace local."

Austin shook his head. "Nah. I realized I'm too much like the stubborn stallions we get sometimes. Or...maybe my father."

"No shit." Jake chuckled at that. "You've always been just like Silas."

"I need space and freedom. Independence. I don't think I can cut it working for someone else. Somehow, I have to do my own thing. Be my own boss or something. Have some sort of control over my own damn life."

"Independence is overrated. Finding your rightful place in the Compass clan, that makes sense to me, though." Jake looked at Austin then. His piercing gaze made it clear this was one of those rare times when he was being dead serious. "There's strength in being part of something like this. A reason I stayed all these years. Throwing it away for something you're not completely committed to would be foolish."

Yes. That's *exactly* how he felt. "Worst of all, I took this girl on a few dates and sort of thought it could get serious, but the only things she cared about were my major and the kinds of jobs I'd get and what neighborhood I wanted to live in."

"Neighborhood? Wouldn't she want her own land? Room to spread out?"

Austin smiled wryly. "Starting to feel like I haven't gone crazy after all. That's what I wondered, too. But apparently not. And when I proposed bringing her back home with me, she flat out laughed in my face. Like I couldn't possibly be serious. That's when I realized I had nothing in common with her and nearly everyone I met. None of the important stuff. She got all fired up about buying a condo and how great it would be not to have a yard to take care of and how she'd save money living on the middle floor, sandwiched between strangers, and soaking up her neighbor's heat in the winter. She even wanted a miniature designer dog she could put in a metal cage during the day with nowhere to roam. I felt like that animal, except I'm more of a mutt. Just as trapped, though. I wasn't made to be someone's pet."

"Nope. Nope. Nope. I understand your point, kid." Jake grimaced. "If you felt this way from the start, why didn't you tell anyone? No one's going to force you to do something that makes you miserable just for a piece of paper."

"My parents. They threw me that huge party when I got

accepted and my dad—Colby—wrote me a long letter about how proud I'd made him. My sister, Clayton, and Wyatt sent me care packages and encouragement around midterms and finals, telling me how well they knew I'd do. They didn't intend to pressure me, I know. Still, when the people you care most about think what you're doing is so wonderful and important but you disagree, it's like standing in the path of a charging herd. Go with them or get trampled." He gritted his teeth. "I didn't want —no, *don't* want—to let them down. But I have. I just couldn't do it anymore. To make it worse, I wasted two damn years of my life."

"You're, what, nineteen now?"

Austin nodded. Almost twenty and starting over. He'd lost too much time chasing someone else's dream.

"I'd kill to be young again." Jake flexed his hands, which seemed more gnarled than ever. His bones cracked and popped as he squeezed his fingers into fists. "Plenty of time to try a couple things and figure out what you're good at and what makes you happy. Hopefully you'll find something that's a bit of both. I've had my own share of failures. Most I made worse by clinging onto a lame horse too long, but at least I know I tried my damnedest to succeed. You'll have that peace of mind. You gave the college thing your best effort. It's important, you know, having no doubts about that. Especially now that I realize exactly how long the rest of your life is. It's terrible to wonder if you could have done just a tiny bit more when it counted."

"Are you talking about Viho's mom?" Austin peered at Jake from the corner of his eye. The cowboy was Austin's cousin Sterling's husband's dad, though none of them—Jake included —had known he had a son for far too long. Now *that* would suck. Missing out on seeing your kid grow up, not having a chance to provide for them like any honorable man at Compass Ranch would do. Losing the love of your life.

Jake hummed softly, "I sure would like a do-over with

Haiwee. Even if it ended the same way, I'd be sure to enjoy my mistakes more. How we fill our days is rarely a waste. You must have gotten something out of your time away from here, right?"

"The parties were fun, for a while." Austin shrugged. "There were more girls around there, too."

"Uh huh. I'm starting to see why you took some time making your mind up." The old man rocked his shoulder into Austin's.

"I'm not going to lie, that was part of it. But it got old pretty quick. Mostly I'm worried about my parents. I don't want to be the loser in a family of overachievers. Shit!" He picked up a stone then threw it over the edge of the ridge. That's how he felt, plummeting toward the hard-packed ground.

Collision inevitable.

"Trust me, after they think on it for a few minutes, your mom, dad, and father are going to say the same things I am. I'll bet you a month of cleaning stalls they'll be more pissed about you hiding it from them than your decision to leave." Jake smacked him on the back of the head. "How long did you think you could stay out here, anyway?"

"Only a couple days more. I'm running low on my mac and cheese stash," Austin admitted.

"Desperate times, kid." Jake laughed at that. "Look, I realize everyone in this whole damn town talks about your papaw JD like he was a saint. I respected him. He was a great boss and an even better friend to me, so don't take this the wrong way."

Austin angled his hat toward the sun so he could peer directly at Jake for the first time. The deep grooves etched into his cheeks and forehead had grown surprisingly more evident since last he'd seen the guy. His hair had transitioned from salt and pepper to snow white at some point when Austin wasn't paying attention. What he said next was even more surprising, though.

"I'm telling you that as incredible as JD was, he wasn't perfect. Nobody is. There were plenty of times he tried something that didn't pan out and other times when we weren't sure if the ranch would make it through a bad season. Droughts, blights, hard winters…I've seen it all on this ranch. What made him great—and same for your father when he took over after his dad—was that he was never quite satisfied. He never stopped looking for a way to make things better. He lifted the people around him up when they were struggling, and made himself pretty damn happy in the process, even if it wasn't in the way he'd originally imagined. I think you're a Compton through and through, kid. You'll figure this out and make it work for you."

"You really think so?" Austin did find that hard to believe. Was Jake just trying to cheer him up?

If so, it was kind of working.

"Yup. Go talk to your parents. Tell them how you really feel. Then get out there and try something else. You're sure as shit not going to do much sitting up here, hiding. My advice, though…at least put a shirt on so they can't see you've gotten a fistful of new tattoos since Christmas." Jake grumbled as he plopped his hat back on his head. "How many of those damn things do you need, anyway?"

"More than I have." Austin grinned as Jake shook his head. "It's not like my parents can say much about that. My father's back piece is epic, like all my uncles'. I'm saving that spot for something really important. Hey, maybe I'll get a portrait of you."

"You little shit, don't you fucking dare." The pure horror on Jake's face made Austin pretty damn sure he would have to consider it seriously.

For the first time in forever, he cracked up. He wiped the corners of his eyes, telling himself the moisture on the side of his hand was only because of his laughing fit.

"It's going to be okay. I promise. I know how much you look up to your folks, kid."

"I do. To you too, Jake." Austin got to his feet then. Jake was right about one thing. Putting it off wasn't helping ease his anxiety. It would be a relief to get this over with and maybe start to move on from this disaster.

In standard cowboy fashion, Jake simply tipped his hat at the compliment.

"Hey, Jake?" Austin asked.

"Yeah?"

"Will you come with me? To tell my parents, I mean."

"Of course, kid." Jake slapped Austin on the shoulder. "Pack this shit up and let's go home."

"You're going to ride back then come out with a truck to get me and all this junk, right?" It was hot as hell out here despite the early hour. Every minute that passed would get worse.

"Nah, your ass can walk for being a coward. Next time, own your shit and come clean as soon as you realize there's a problem. It's always easier that way. Hustle, too. Since you're here, you might as well help with the chores."

"Yes, sir." Austin spun on his heel and got to work tearing down his campsite. At least he could be useful. Maybe Jake knew he needed that right now.

Austin Compton honked the air horn of the gleaming big rig he drove. The roar of the beastly semi's engine drowned out the shouts of Jake and the rest of the ranch hands, who'd just finished loading the livestock trailer. He didn't need to hear them to know they were wishing him and their precious cargo a safe trip to its new home, a feedlot a few states over.

He waved goodbye to his mom, dad, and father on his way through the yard, then bounced along the gravel road that led out of Compass Ranch. It would take him a week or so to make the round trip to deliver the batch of barely weaned calves he was towing.

Careful turning onto the main road, Austin tried his best to keep from stressing his young passengers. They were more resilient than the fully grown cattle he took to processing plants at the end of the season and less finicky than the fancy-shmancy horses he delivered for Uncle Seth in the off months. They required a hell of a lot more care and attention than hay bales, though.

Austin spent a good portion of his time transporting their

spare crop of feed to whatever part of the country was having a drought that particular year. Uncle Sam, who managed the ranch finances, figured the profit on the marked-up hay alone paid for the rest of Austin's delivery services, which were a major convenience for smaller operations. Offering them gave Compass Ranch a competitive advantage. In the time since Austin had bailed on college, convinced his parents to spend his tuition on the down payment for a truck, and started driving the rig instead of suffering through additional education he'd never use, he'd increased their out-of-state business by thirty-seven percent.

It felt good to have carved out his own niche for helping the ranch prosper and earning his keep.

Jake liked to gloat about how he'd called it and continually pointed out how Austin was too much like his father to get beat down by one mistake. Austin figured that was mostly a compliment. Sure, Silas could be more obstinate than the ranch's crankiest jackass. But he was also hardworking, strong, and loyal to his family. He'd sacrifice anything necessary to make sure the people he loved were happy and well taken care of—even if they wanted a hundred-thousand-dollar truck after blowing nearly half that on tuition for a degree they'd never finish.

Of course, Austin had paid every penny back with interest.

Austin didn't mind a hard day's work. It suited him better than studying had. He'd leave that bookworm shit to his cousin, the future Dr. Bryant Compton, who was nearly finished with his PhD in sustainability engineering, whatever the fuck that meant.

His sister, Hope, and the rest of his girl cousins had settled comfortably into life in Compton Pass. Hell, Sterling's daughter was nearly eleven now. The boys in his generation were another story. Bryant, Doug, and James sent Austin pitying looks over their videochats when he left home on one of his long-haul trips. They couldn't understand the appeal of sleeping in the truck and staring at the stars, or the allure of the open road.

Secretly, Austin lived for his excursions. It was a happy medium between getting out and seeing some of the world on his own yet always knowing the ranch—and his enormous, crazy-ass family—was there, waiting for his return.

He didn't need to be a fire jumper like James or a storm chaser like Doug to get his thrills, or a genius water conservation expert-in-training like Bryant to feel like he was making a difference. A long drive, a couple cold beers at a seedy bar, exchanging stories with people he'd just met, and the occasional one-night fling with a girl looking for a wild time were good enough for him.

Maybe that made him simple. If so, he didn't give a fuck.

Austin rolled down the windows, cranked up the radio, and began singing at the top of his lungs while warm late-spring air buffeted his face. He grinned as he snaked along the highway, taking in the gorgeous Wyoming mountains that towered over the plains.

Soon they'd level out as he left the Rockies behind, where they'd be waiting patiently for his not-too-distant return.

Yep. This was the life.

2

———

Uneven boot-steps clomped across the squeaky porch, waking Hayden from the fitful sleep she'd dropped in and out of while waiting for Bobby Joe to come home. Dread and relief warred within her. At least he wasn't splattered across a back road somewhere. Soon she might not be very grateful for that, though.

She glanced at the time on her bedside clock. After midnight.

That could only mean one thing. He was drunk again. It was late enough that he'd be past the fun stages of inebriation. Nah, he would be well into the darker side of his addiction by now. The worst parts of him—angry, bitter, mean, petty, aggressive—would be on full display. *Shit.*

Hayden braced herself.

Fumes potent enough to blow up their cabin, especially if sparked by either of their tempers, assaulted her nose the moment he ripped open the door, letting it crash against the rickety clapboard. The acrid bite of illegal, homemade moonshine—the cheapest shit he could lay his hands on— made her eyes water. She swore that stuff was making him crazy. Who knew what kind of chemicals Cletus Johnson and his brothers were putting into that junk to get people smashed for a fraction of the cost of alcohol produced to any reasonable standard?

Bobby Joe staggered inside without bothering to lock up. Keeping her safe, never mind happy, was no longer his priority. He lurched to one side. Attempting to remove his boot resulted in him crashing to the floor like a giant tree falling in a storm. He didn't even put his hands out to stop his face-plant.

Definitely hammered.

Pretending to be out cold was the only defensive maneuver she had. So she gave it a go. Hayden curled into a ball and slammed her eyes shut, trying not to tremble hard enough to make the metal bedframe squeak. Unfortunately, her act wasn't very believable. Bobby Joe could have woken the dead in the family cemetery behind the one-room shanty they rented from the rancher next door. His cursing escalated as he struggled to his knees then crawled the rest of the way toward the corner of the glorified shed they had called home these past five years.

Things hadn't always been awful. Sure, they'd never had money to spare. Two local kids with high school diplomas and not much else, who swore they'd make it together despite the odds against them and everyone's doubts. Gossipy bullshit didn't matter to her. She'd imagined they were like those trendy couples living adventurously in tiny homes because they craved a minimalist lifestyle, not because that was their only option.

People's opinions mattered to Bobby Joe, though. After his glory days as the town's football star were over, he hadn't adjusted very well to being a regular schmuck like the rest of them. He expected people to revere him, clear the way for him, like his teachers had when his grades had fallen short of the athletics program requirements without a bit of extra credit sprinkled over his late and half-assed assignments.

Hayden had gladly worked three jobs, including scrubbing

toilets at the skeevy roadside motel near the highway, as he searched for something worthy of his time.

Nearly a year after graduation, he'd finally accepted a junior salesman position at the town's used car lot. Bobby Joe didn't appreciate being the low man on the totem pole, even if he sucked at the job. Bitterness plagued him, souring the small victories they might have otherwise celebrated while building a better life together.

Hayden had done her damnedest to keep them afloat despite his constant negativity. It weighed on her, dragging her down to the depths of his misery more often than she cared to admit. She hugged herself, squeezing her fingers over the reminder she'd had tattooed along her side. Maybe it was time to bail. She wasn't quite ready, but maybe she never truly would be. After he'd passed out, she could make her move. How had it come to this?

It hadn't been long before Bobby Joe would detour to the bar on his way home from not-selling cars. A few beers with the guys after work or on game days had turned into something more dangerous than that over time. Constant pressures on their finances, made worse by his nights out and his half-empty attitude, exacerbated their problems.

These days, Hayden had to think hard to recall what she'd seen in him from the start. No matter how desperately she'd clung to the goofy, happy-go-lucky winner Bobby Joe had once been, that boy she'd fallen in love with had slipped away. It was time to admit that she'd lost him for good.

I guess those people and their nasty whispers were right after all.

At least she'd tried. Given their relationship her absolute best, despite the ulcer she suspected it had given her. She couldn't say for sure because they hadn't had the cash for her to see the doctor even if she could have gotten the time off to schedule an appointment at the town's clinic. Each of her employers gave her almost-but-not-quite enough hours to qualify for medical insurance benefits, and since she and Bobby Joe had never gotten married like they'd once dreamed about—*thank God*—he couldn't add her to his coverage.

Hayden probably should have left a long, long time ago. But she'd given it her all. And she'd failed. Despite her best efforts to be silent, a frustrated, miserable groan escaped her.

Bobby Joe took that as a sign that she was awake enough for him to harass. He kneed her ribs as he climbed into their bed, still fully dressed. "Don't even wait up for your man anymore, do you?"

She clutched her side, rocking as stars illuminated the inky field behind her eyelids, trying to convince herself it had been an accident. He was too intoxicated to have aimed that well, right?

Anger frothed through her. When would it be enough? The excuses, the self-doubt, her blaming herself for everything? Tonight. That's when. She was fucking over it all. Over. It.

Hayden sat up gingerly then glared at Bobby Joe. "You're the one who chose not to come home."

Honestly, she was glad he hadn't. It meant less time she'd had to spend faking a smile or gritting her teeth. It exhausted her to guarantee every anodyne comment she made couldn't possibly offend while still scrutinizing his every move, hyperaware of his mood as she waited for their next argument to erupt.

"Don't act so innocent." He shoved her shoulder, definitely *not* by chance.

Hayden tumbled to her back on the thin, saggy mattress they'd shared since before he'd lost himself to alcohol and the gloom he carried inside him.

"What the fuck have I done except bust my ass so you could chug what little money we had?" Fuck this. Most times lately she refused to be lured into a fight, thinking of the long game. Tonight she couldn't take another minute of his bullshit.

He might not know it, but she had a plan.

"What have you done? Every fucking guy that comes on to you at the diner, I bet," he snarled, flinging spittle across her face with his slurred accusation.

"What?" She wiped it away with the back of her hand, blinking. Stunned. Where would he get an idea like that?

He was the one who'd cheated on her. Probably lots of times.

Hayden hadn't bothered calling him on it, afraid of rousing his ire when she'd already decided to leave him. The DNA test she'd seen was enough proof for her that the woman who'd marched into her section at the diner a month or so ago and claimed to be having Bobby Joe's baby was a lot more likely to be telling the truth than her scumbag boyfriend.

"You've been holding out on me." He gripped her upper arm then, crushing it between his fingers as he shook her hard enough to make her bite her own tongue. "Could have at least let me watch, whore."

"You're so fucking drunk you're hallucinating. Making shit up. Let me go!" She yanked but couldn't wrest her arm free of his hold. Icy fear prickled along her spine.

The tang of iron blossoming across her tongue nearly distracted her until Bobby Joe bellowed, "Not until you tell me where you got all that cash!"

"I don't know what you're talking about." A lie. A big fat whopper. She'd never been good at telling them, but if ever there was a time to fib, it was then. Her stomach bottomed out. If he'd found her stash, she might be in real danger. There'd be no way out and she'd just crossed some major lines, pissed Bobby Joe off like never before.

Truth was, Hayden had been playing open mic nights for tips while he'd assumed she was tucked in at home. For months he'd gotten drunk in the woods with his loser buddies and she'd padded the space beneath a loose floorboard in the corner with cash. Her goal was to save enough for a bus ticket to Anywhere Else, USA, and a few months of rent on a cheap but safe enough place to start getting her life in order.

Things had spiraled out of control gradually enough at first that she'd kept thinking she could reverse their downward trajectory. Once she'd realized it was too late, around the time Bobby Joe had started spending most of his nights out, it had really gone to shit fast.

Hayden hated the things she'd done to keep the peace until she could plot her escape. She winced thinking of how she'd lain still beneath Bobby Joe while he got himself off, relying on brute force when it was clear she wasn't into fucking him. If he demanded that of her again tonight, she thought she might be sick. So maybe it was better to come clean.

"Good, then you won't bitch at me for spending the money I found down there." He flung his arm out. It wobbled like a limp noodle in the direction of her hiding spot.

"No!" She wrenched away from him, slipping from his uncoordinated hold. It had taken her weeks to amass even that pittance, and he'd destroyed it in a few hours. He would do the same to her if she hung around any longer.

She was leaving. Hayden had sworn to herself that she was. It just took time to make that a reality. She'd had to be so careful not to get caught. Not to tip him off.

Now it had been for nothing.

"Guess you're not such a goody two-shoes after all." His face turned purple.

Hayden probably should have expected it. But she didn't.

The crack of his fist against her cheekbone ricocheted through her skull. It was the final straw. Primal instincts roared to life within her. She kicked and punched, flailed and bucked until she got lucky.

Her knee crashed into Bobby Joe's balls. Hard.

The bastard curved in on himself and squirmed around on

his back like a turtle that couldn't right itself. Instead of wasting her breath screaming at him or throwing away this chance, which she would likely never have again, Hayden ran.

Since that bastard had spent her escape kitty, she didn't even have to pause to dig the folded bills from beneath the loose floorboards before she fled into the night.

Bobby Joe's shouts echoed around her, making her shiver a lot more violently than the cool spring air that slapped her throbbing face.

The pain inspired her to keep sprinting despite her bare feet, which were being sliced to shreds on the pricker bushes she smashed through. She scaled the fence to the rancher's property and toppled over it, adding a few scrapes and gouges to her list of injuries. None of them were as painful as the ones to her pride.

How had she let things come to this? Never again.

She would never depend on a man again. Never tie herself to someone so tightly that she disappeared in his shadow.

Hayden cut through tall grass and pastures. Maybe she'd knock on the door of the main house and beg for shelter. They'd probably insist on calling the police. Cops weren't likely to help, though. They knew Bobby Joe, had cheered for him. A few still hung out with him and turned a blind eye to the activities going down in the woods in exchange for bottomless free samples.

No, Bobby Joe still had more fans in town than her.

If they delivered her into Bobby Joe's clutches, she didn't think he would let her go again. The embarrassment of being dumped would be intolerable to his fragile ego.

No one knew that side of him like she did.

Hayden didn't have a single dollar in her pocket. Or even a goddamned pocket for that matter. She had an oversized T-shirt that she usually slept in. No shoes, no coat, no underwear.

Fucked, that's what she was.

If she could make it through the night, she could wait for Bobby Joe to go to work then sneak back in and grab a few necessities. She'd figure out what to do from there. One step at a time, she would do this. She had no other choice.

First thing she needed was a place to go to ground for a few hours.

Hayden paused and listened. No more shouts reached her ears. Bobby Joe had been far too impaired to make it this far without breaking a leg, she was pretty sure. So she crept over to the barn that housed her neighbor's livestock. Except no matter how hard she yanked, she couldn't open the door.

Locked? Damn it.

A warm glow and the boisterous voices of the ranch hands spilled from the windows of the bunkhouse. She kept a wide berth as she slunk around it. Though they sounded like much more pleasant drunks than Bobby Joe, she'd learned her lesson. It was wise to stay away from trouble before it got out of hand.

Up ahead, a cherry-red semi with an ornate compass rose painted on the side was hitched to a livestock trailer. She'd seen it roll through town earlier this afternoon. If it was still here, that meant its owner would be spending the night.

Hayden peeked inside. Whoever had been driving it had taken the time to clean it out meticulously. The only thing remaining inside was a neat pile of fresh hay the animals hadn't eaten en route. Right then, it looked like heaven on earth.

She glanced around. Everyone was inside.

If she could rest for a while, she'd be able to creep away before first light and hide somewhere else until she spied Bobby Joe pulling out of their dirt driveway with one of the cars he perpetually borrowed from the lot since they couldn't afford one of their own.

No one would know she'd been there.

Hayden hopped into the trailer and crept toward the front. She rearranged the hay in the corner, using it to form a nest.

Some of it she tucked beneath her to act as a buffer from the cold metal while the rest she fluffed over her bare legs. Thank goodness the worst of the cold nights were behind them.

She drew her knees to her chin and wrapped her arms around her shins. When she rested her forehead on her legs, pain radiated around her eye.

Do. Not. Cry.

She couldn't risk alerting anyone to her presence. Neither did she want to exacerbate the zings stabbing her side and arm in time to her pounding heartbeat.

Besides, she'd shed plenty of tears over her bad judgment.

Bobby Joe had hurt her enough. She'd never let him or anyone else do that to her again.

3

A maroon dragon flapped its wings then swooped from the stormy sky in Hayden's direction, teeth bared. She screamed and dodged as it breathed flames that licked her cheek, ribs, and feet. At least they also warmed her a bit. Why was she running across a glacier in her nightshirt anyway?

Another rumble, this one decidedly more mechanical than animal.

When she looked over her shoulder again a giant robotic Bobby Joe chased her, its eyes glowing like embers. A loud hiss followed. Was the dragon circling around? She'd be trapped between the two monsters.

Hayden tumbled to the side as the ground shook.

When her sore arm hit the freezing ground, she finally roused from the nightmares plaguing her to an even more grim reality.

It was still dark when she jolted awake. She cowered in the corner of a cold-as-fuck metal box, her gaze darting frantically around her. Hayden couldn't make out much, but it was enough to know she was not in her bed.

The whoosh of an air brake made it clear what had inspired the dragon of her dreams.

Fuck! It came back to her in a rush.

She'd hidden in that gleaming livestock trailer attached to the mammoth semi from out of state. The one now rolling with her still in it, jostling her with every bump down the unpaved road leading off her neighbor's ranch. By the time she fully realized what was happening, they'd hit the main street and picked up some speed. She could probably jump off, tuck and roll, flashing her ass to anyone around. Or pray that he got stopped by the town's single traffic light before easing onto the highway.

But then where would she be? Homeless, broke, and in danger of crossing paths with Bobby Joe before she could come up with some other way out of this shithole town.

Fate could be trying to tell her something. Maybe she should listen. Take the free ride.

At the first real stop the truck made, she could bail, try to find a homeless shelter that might have some donated clothes, then beg for work or hitch to somewhere farther away. Somewhere she could begin again.

It was going to be uncomfortable. Staying would be unbearable.

So she clung to the metal bars, gritted her teeth against the wind already whipping through the open sides of the trailer, and prayed for the sun to come up as quickly as possible.

What felt like years but was probably only a few hours later, Hayden's teeth chattered uncontrollably. She'd started eyeing the extra bale of hay a while back when her bladder began to protest. It was becoming an emergency situation.

Didn't the guy driving this thing need some damn coffee like a normal human being? Maybe he had a fucking thermos. She would kill for a sip from it right now. Hell, she'd blow a stranger at the truck stop just to wrap her fingers around his hot drink for a minute or two.

Fine. Didn't he need a post-coffee poop break after guzzling all that warm, delicious, caffeinated liquid? Something, come on!

Anything to get her out of this mobile jail cell. Her entire body ached, even the parts the sunshine piercing between the aluminum slatted walls of the trailer didn't highlight as bruised or swollen. It was official. She despised Bobby Joe and what he'd become, and especially what he'd done to her.

When the truck decelerated and took an exit, Hayden crossed her fingers and her toes in addition to her legs, which were already squeezed tight to prevent an accident.

She psyched herself up for what she had to do. As they slowed further, she struggled to stand and attempted taking a few steps to work out the kinks in every muscle in her body. Her legs shook. Why hadn't she worn sweats or even some leggings to bed the night before?

How was she going to explain being half-naked when they got wherever the hell they were going? She was about to find out.

The rig rolled to a stop. One final jerk and they were *finally* stationary. Holy hell.

Her ears rang without the rush of air, the whir of the tires on the pavement, or the surprisingly loud noise of passing cars. How did cattle manage to survive a ride like this? The experience might turn her into a vegetarian, though right then she would have been glad for a few cows to snuggle up to.

Hayden peeked between the rows of metal to see if the coast was clear. The truck's driver, who seemed younger, tougher, and definitely hotter than she'd imagined, moseyed inside the station to pay for his fuel or maybe finally empty his *gigantic* bladder.

She'd never been so jealous of a person using a gas station bathroom in her whole life.

Though her oblivious savior had turned out to be a heck of a lot finer than she'd imagined in his well-worn jeans, fashionable cowboy hat with matching boots, and sleeveless orange-and-blue plaid work shirt, which put an array of fierce tattoos on display, he also seemed like the kind of man she didn't care to mess with. One as dangerous—and very likely more capable—than Bobby Joe. One who might not appreciate her joy ride in his trailer. Time to go.

Steadying herself with one hand on the wall, she inched toward the side door.

Looking around furiously, she figured this would be about as good of a chance as she'd get. But right before she slipped out, another truck turned into the lot. They pulled directly on the other side of the pump from where she stood.

Shit! Shit! Shit!

It wasn't like she could walk out of here and act like it was no big deal. A woman so inappropriately dressed was going to draw some attention. When someone cracked some snide joke about her trucker's bare-assed lady friend, he was going to have some questions she didn't particularly care to answer.

Had she broken any laws by stowing away in this rig? How understanding would he, his boss, or the cops be if she busted out of here covered in hay and not much else? Would he take matters into his own hands and use her situation to his advantage? More likely, the authorities would cart her off straight to a psych ward. At the very least, they'd probably arrest her. She didn't have money for bail or anyone to call to come get her. She couldn't afford trouble.

Gritting her teeth, she glanced longingly at the nice warm station and the cute diner attached, where she might be able to take on the shittiest duties to earn a hot meal, then back at the freezing corner of the trailer, where she'd hunkered down for a couple hundred miles.

She'd done it once. She could do it again...right?

No choice. Because here came handsome driver dude while the newcomer was still fueling up.

Hayden crawled back to her straw, gathered it up as best she could, then dove beneath it for camouflage.

Silent tears fell down her cheeks as she made herself as small and invisible as possible until the truck began to move once more. She bawled as she relieved herself on a few handfuls of straw like the animal Bobby Joe had turned her into. Then she threw it out the side of the trailer, reducing what little insulation she had from the elements.

Once she had the cover of darkness, or they pulled off the major highway onto a road with more cover where the driver would reduce his speed, she'd ditch her ride.

Until then, she simply held on.

4

Hayden couldn't believe it.

After one of the most miserable days of her life, filled with physical discomfort and nothing except time to dwell on how she'd hit rock bottom, she'd done it. She'd actually escaped both Bobby Joe and the intimidating cowboy trucker who'd helped her cross state lines.

When her unsuspecting getaway driver had wandered into a roadside bar and grill, she'd burst from his trailer in an uncoordinated flurry of limbs that had resulted in adding a skinned knee to her collection of minor injuries. Before she could head for the tree line on the other side of the parking lot and figure out her next step, she noticed that he'd left his jacket where he'd draped it through one of the slats in the side wall of the trailer before making his full-circuit inspection of the vehicle a few minutes ago.

Her heart still pounded from the sheer terror his nearness had brought. What if he had turned his head just a little as he'd stooped near the tire she'd hid behind? He'd been only inches away, close enough to reach out and touch, before he'd completed his due diligence and ambled inside.

Would she go to hell if she took his coat, given the circumstances?

If a starving man stole a loaf of bread, was it still wrong? Yeah, probably. But she'd cut him a break. Hopefully the universe agreed and would do the same for her.

Her fingers hovered over the supple leather, stroking it once before snatching her hand back.

Hayden bit her lip as she studied the smattering of gnarled pines she'd likely be spending the night in. She silently swore she'd donate ten jackets to a homeless shelter the instant she could afford to. Then she grabbed the coat and flung it around her shoulders.

Oh God. It was still warm and smelled incredible.

Better yet, when she stuck her hands in the pockets, they weren't empty. Her fingers closed around something hard and round. When she withdrew her fist, she nearly wept again, this time from joy. An apple. A juicy, red, tempting apple.

Though she probably should have run first and eaten later, she couldn't stop herself from taking a bite right then and there. One taste didn't satisfy her. She took another. When her other hand retrieved a granola bar from the second pocket, she ripped it open with her teeth and inhaled some of that too.

She grinned and took it as another sign that karma was rewarding her. Things were going to be okay.

Somehow.

Hayden clutched her prizes as she bolted toward the woods.

Unfortunately, she hadn't made it even a quarter of the way there when a man's shout boomed through the night like thunder. "Hey!"

It might have been a sexy voice if it hadn't been so damned scary. It had to belong to the tattooed badass who drove the red compass truck.

Uh oh.

She took off, pumping her arms in an attempt to speed

herself up. Unfortunately, this guy wasn't drunk like Bobby Joe had been. His long strides were impossible to outrun, especially when barefoot, stiff, and battered from a wild journey. Not to mention the events of the night before.

Hayden refused to surrender. She kept putting one foot in front of the other until a strong arm wrapped around her middle and lifted her clear off the ground. "Where do you think you're going with *my* jacket?"

She dropped her breakfast, lunch, and dinner, freeing her hands to fight him off as best as she could.

5

Austin peered over the top of the menu in the direction of his rig. He squinted, then scrubbed his hands over his face. It had been a long haul. His tired eyes were blurry around the edges. He must be seeing things.

Otherwise, how could he make sense of the sexy-as-fuck pair of legs walking away with what looked like his lucky leather jacket? Had he left it flung over the trailer hitch after finishing his end-of-the-day checklist?

Shit.

He shoved out of the booth. As he passed the waitress, she asked, "Everything okay?"

"Just fine," he responded with a disarming smile. It would be, as soon as he took care of this situation. "I'd like a bacon cheeseburger with fries. And a beer. Make that two. Be right back."

"Sure thing, sweetie." She popped her gum then sized him up as if she'd like to take a bite out of him.

Annoyed at being distracted from one of the highlights of his time on the road—flirting with women who didn't expect more than a night of fun—he slammed his palms on the doors of the restaurant. He took off at a jog, picking up speed when he realized the woman absconding with his coat was deceptively quick and light on her feet.

As he charged toward the would-be thief, he yelled, "Hey!"

Unsurprisingly, she didn't respond or slow down. Despite her lack of shoes—or pants, for that matter—she ran fast enough to set her long chestnut brown hair blowing in the wind.

When he caught up to her, Austin grabbed her around her tiny waist and hauled her backward against his chest. "Where do you think you're going with *my* jacket?"

The woman in his hold freaked the fuck out. She shrieked and thrashed, dropping the apple and granola bar he'd completely forgotten about, minus a bite or two out of each. What the fuck?

What was she doing out here with hardly anything on, starving half to death?

"Whoa. Settle down." Austin switched his hold, nabbing the thief by the collar of his jacket and the T-shirt she wore beneath. She swam in the thing. It would have been impossible for her to slip free, but he gave her the illusion of freedom. When he let her stand on her own, she wobbled. He tightened his grip so she couldn't fall. "What's going on here?"

"I—" She angled toward him and tried to respond, but it seemed like her teeth were chattering too much for her to get out more than a word or two at a time. Despite the blue tinge to her lips, he couldn't help but notice how fucking gorgeous she was, even if he hadn't let his stare wander from her face to her bare, sexy legs.

When she swiped her hair from her face and glared at him fully, he could hardly breathe. Partly because she was easily the prettiest girl he'd ever seen. Mostly because one hell of a shiner marred her natural beauty. Any flicker of arousal died the moment he realized the shadows that darkened both her eyes were much deeper on one side than the other. As he examined the rest of her, he realized her neck, legs, feet, and fingers were also smudged with the evidence of a struggle.

She winced when his tightening muscles inadvertently jerked her off balance.

Damn.

Freckles dotted the tan skin of her cheeks and the bridge of her pert nose. Brown eyes bored into his with a combination of defiance, bravado, and determination that turned him on. Or would have if the situation hadn't been quite so fucked up.

He had to get to the bottom of this.

Austin used his grip to steer his pretty little crook toward the cab of his truck.

"I'm sorry. Please don't hurt me or call the cops. I shouldn't have taken your stuff, eaten your food. I'm sorry. I've never stolen anything before in my life. Hell, I've never even gotten a parking ticket." She seemed to collapse in on herself then before rasping, "This isn't the kind of person I am. I swear."

He recalled the death-grip she'd had on the apple he'd been too full to eat during his afternoon snack. The reality of the situation began to sink in. This woman, whoever she was, needed help. His anger melted away in the face of her desperation.

The frantic whip of her gaze in every direction but his made him sure, though, that if he let go, she would bolt before he could do any good. He didn't want to scare her by chasing her again or add to her discomfort by tackling her to the rough pavement when she had nothing protecting her bare skin—creamy, soft skin—from the waist down.

So he braced himself for her resistance, then scooped her into his arms.

Sure enough, she went ballistic again.

"Hold still. I'm not pissed," he promised. "It looks like you could use a few minutes in the truck with the heat on. Why don't you come inside and tell me what you're doing out here dressed—well, *undressed*—like that?"

The woman he held might have been petite, but she sure was strong. She bucked like the unbroken fillies they had on Compass Ranch from time to time. The kind he loved to tame and ride.

Now was not the time to think about that.

The last thing he should do was get a hard-on. That would creep her out for sure. He wasn't trying to lure her into his truck so he could do terrible things to her. How was she to know that?

"Get off me! I'm not going anywhere with you. I changed my mind—call the cops. Right now."

To be honest, he would rip his sister or any of his female cousins a new one if they did what he'd just proposed. "Sorry. I'm putting you down, okay?"

After making his way back to the truck, Austin set her on her feet and slowly released his hold. Even still, she staggered before catching her balance. She might have thrashed like a mountain lion caught in a trap, but she was clearly freezing. Exhausted. Injured. Ready to topple.

"Did one of the other drivers kick you out or something?" He took stock of the parking lot, finding it as sparsely occupied as he'd remembered. Two of the rigs belonged to guys he knew in passing. That didn't mean they didn't take advantage of some of the women who congregated in truck stops, offering their companionship—and more—on the road. But if they treated them like this, their faces would be meeting his fist next time he saw them.

She shook her head, staring at the ground, as if trying to figure out a way to flee.

Even if Austin let her leave, where would she go? There was nothing around. Speaking of... "Then how'd you get out here? We're in the middle of a fucking national forest. It's got to be at least thirty miles to the nearest town. Did you seriously walk all that way without shoes or most of your clothes?"

She bit her lower lip and looked skyward, as if asking for divine guidance.

"Try the truth," he suggested. "It's easier than making shit up."

The woman sighed. The noise was the exasperated sort he'd heard often from his sister when she dealt with her husbands or any of the other Compass men. Then she said, "I came with you."

"What?" His jaw dropped. She couldn't mean... "Holy fuck! My last stop was nearly two states ago. You were in the back that whole time? Is *that* how you got so banged up?"

"Not exactly." She grimaced.

"Jesus, if you didn't get hurt in the back of my truck, who did this to you? Did someone see you in there? Jump you? Take advantage—" Austin's fists clenched as he looked around the truck stop. If the bastard who'd laid his hands on her was still there, he'd make sure the guy thought long and hard before abusing another woman.

Hayden flinched.

The last thing Austin wanted was to frighten her, so he forced himself to relax. His fingers unclenched one by one. "Is he out there?" He jerked his chin toward the inky lot dotted with halos of light from the overhead lamps.

She shook her head no.

It was hard to say if her full-body quivering had more to do with the chill evening air or her fear, but he figured the least he could do was warm her up while he figured out what the fuck was going on. Austin yanked open the passenger side door. He set one boot on the running board and reached for his thermos. After unscrewing the top, which doubled as a cup, he filled it to the brim with the extra-strong coffee he guzzled to help keep himself alert on the road.

He held it out to her. "Here. Take this."

She lunged forward. When her fingers wrapped around his, he hissed. "Damn, you're freezing."

Without bothering to respond, she took a long sip from the metal, then another. Still, she didn't talk. His patience wore thin.

"You'd better explain what you were doing in the trailer." He folded his arms.

She retreated a step. "I didn't do it on purpose, I swear. I got in a fight with my boyfriend last night. It was bad. *Really* bad."

"I can see that." His attempt at reining in his fury at the sight of her bruised skin was pretty much a flop.

"I didn't have anywhere to go. So I hid in the hay back there, thinking I could lay low until my boyfriend went to work today. Except I fell asleep."

"Hang on. You were in the truck for almost twenty-four hours? Since before I took off this morning?" Horrified, he imagined a much different ending to the day. One where he discovered her lifeless body in the back of his truck. Son of a bitch!

She swallowed hard and nodded.

"Damn it!" He groaned. "You could have been killed."

"Believe me, I know. I didn't plan to stay. You left early. When I woke up we were already moving. And I thought..." She started to hyperventilate.

"You thought it would be a quick way to put some distance between you and the fucker who hurt you." Austin lightly cupped his hand over hers under the pretense of refilling her cup.

She drank deep, then nodded. "I didn't have a choice. I'm so sorry I used you like that."

"Are you okay? Do you need me to call a doctor?" He still couldn't believe she'd endured the entire trip in the trailer. "My ass is sore from that haul and I was sitting on a throne compared to you. That had to have been miserable."

"I peed on your hay," she admitted, blushing furiously. At least some life seemed to return to her now that she'd absorbed warmth from his coffee.

Austin couldn't help it. He cracked up, clutching his gut. "I think that's the least of our worries, honey."

"I really am sorry I got you involved." Hayden downed the last drop and screwed the lid on his thermos. She handed it to him with a wistful sigh and began to slip her arms from his jacket, revealing even more ugly patches of discoloration. "Let me go and I won't bother you anymore."

Fuck that. Austin grabbed the coat, preventing her from fully removing it. He replaced it around her shoulders. She needed it a hell of a lot more than he did. Besides, it looked great on her. "Keep it."

"If you don't mind giving some psycho woman your address, I'll mail it back to you or send you money to buy a new one as soon as I can," she offered, making up his mind to do something outrageous.

His gut screamed at him that if he didn't, he would regret it for the rest of his life.

Not to mention that his mother would kick his ass if he didn't do the right thing and help this woman. For once, maybe, he could live up to the Compass legacy.

"Here." He jammed his hand in his jeans, then held out his keys to her. "Get in the cab. Lock the doors with me and everyone else outside. Crank the heat up. There's a pretty comfy bed in there. Crawl under the covers. You'll be safe. Alone. Take a nap if you think you can relax enough to doze off. I'm gonna go eat my supper in the diner and leave you in peace for a while. It seems like you could use it."

"That thing cost more than what I can make in ten years waiting tables. How do you know I'm not going to try to steal that too? She jacked her thumb over her shoulder toward his rig and shot him a purely female, raised-brow look. The woman waved his keys away. "Are you nuts?"

"I'm not the one who rode in a fucking livestock trailer for over six hundred miles today." He shrugged. "Do you know how to drive a semi?"

"No. I don't even know how to drive a regular stick." Her shoulders slumped, making him wish she'd be open to accepting a hug. She seemed like she needed one.

"Then I don't think you'll steal my truck. Go on." He jingled the keys in her direction. "If you need something, honk the horn and I'll come out."

"Seriously?" She nibbled her lip, which is when he noticed exactly how swollen it was. Fuck. It'd be best if he walked away for a bit to cool down and figure out what to do next. How to handle the situation from there.

"Yeah." He dropped the keys in her palm and couldn't resist letting his fingers brush over hers, happy to feel they had thawed a bit. Too bad she wasn't in any condition mentally or physically to let him share his body heat with her. There were much more pleasant ways to get their blood pumping. "What should I bring you? I mean, I'd invite you in, but they have a no pants, no service rule. Pretty sure I saw a sign like that on the door."

Her jaw dropped. She blinked her innocent and appreciative doe eyes at him, but she didn't respond for a few heartbeats. Then she cracked the faintest of smiles. "Smartass."

"No, seriously, what do you want to eat? It's the least I can do since I made you waste that apple. You like steak? A salad? A bacon cheeseburger and some greasy-ass fries?"

She licked her lips at that last one.

Despite the crazy situation, he chuckled. "That's what I ordered myself. You got it. Don't open the door for anyone but me. Understand?"

When she nodded, he spun on his boot heel and headed back inside, afraid that if he stayed longer it might become impossible to leave. His unexpected guest drew him in, made him wonder what her full story was. How he might keep making things better for her because damn, that felt good.

Ah, shit.

He might need some advice from his cousins on this one.

"Hey," she called softly when he'd taken a couple of steps away.

Her strained voice shot straight to his dick. It sounded like it might if she invited him back to bed after a night spent making her scream with pleasure. His head whipped around fast enough he thought his hat might fly off. "Yeah?"

"Thank you," she whispered, then hurried toward the cab of his truck, as if he might be dumb enough to change his mind. With her back turned, he thought he heard a faint sniffle.

It took every bit of his gentlemanly willpower to leave before watching her climb into his rig so that he could tell if she was wearing anything beneath that old, faded shirt of hers.

For once, his mother would be proud.

6

————

"What's wrong?" Bryant asked as soon as the group videochat connected. He shoved his glasses up his nose and peered into his laptop's screen. In the background, his tiny off-campus apartment was filled with textbooks and a whiteboard covered in scribbled equations as well as notes for an upcoming exam. Thank God that wasn't Austin's life anymore.

James cursed. "Cuz, calm down. Why do you always assume the worst?"

Those two of Austin's cousins were pretty much polar opposites. James dove out of planes to fight fires for a living while Bryant researched water conservation and eco-friendly agricultural advancements from the clinical surroundings of his academic laboratory in pursuit of his PhD. Despite the situation, Austin was happy he was back in the diner instead of in a school.

"Because Austin doesn't call us all at the same time unless something dramatic is happening," Doug chimed in. He fell somewhere between the other two extremes, sort of like Austin. He was still figuring out exactly what he planned to do with his life but seemed to be enjoying his latest stint as a cameraman for a weather channel special on violent storms.

"Good point," James conceded. "What's up?"

"So, there's this girl—" Austin tried to explain.

Doug cut him off. "These conversations always start with lady trouble, don't they? Maybe we should wise up and stick to dudes, like Bryant."

"My love life isn't exactly worth bragging about." Their nerdy cousin frowned.

"That's because you're too busy studying to have fun." Doug shook his head. "You might be smarter than me, but you also might stay a born-again virgin until your dick shrivels up and falls off if you don't start going out again once in a while."

"Guys," Austin interrupted. It was that or listen to them bicker all night. Truth be told, he longed for the times they'd done just that, when they'd all been on Compass Ranch, before they'd flown the coop to do their own things. Holidays were great, but always too short. Growing up together, sharing everything, had been amazing.

They'd done their boy stuff while their older sisters had their own tight-knit club. Now Austin was the only one holding down the fort—or the farm—for Team Compass Boys at the moment. James wouldn't be back again until his time with the West Yellowstone Smoke Jumpers was up in the early fall. Whatever. Either way, it got kind of lonely without these fuckers around to annoy him constantly.

And right now he needed their advice.

"Okay, sorry." James held his hands up. "Focusing."

"This girl...is she hot?" Doug wondered. "Just trying to get the full picture, you know."

"Of course she is or he wouldn't even be considering getting involved in whatever mess he's probably already stepped in." James laughed.

"Jesus. I'm not that shallow," Austin snarled. "She's in

trouble. Someone fucking beat her up and she stowed away in the trailer. I want to help her and I'm not sure how. But yes, she's pretty. She's not wearing any makeup or trying to be beautiful. She's the kind of girl who just is."

"Oh boy." Bryant shook his head.

"I know." Austin scrubbed his hands through his hair. "Trust me, she's not in any sort of position for me—or anyone else—to be hitting on her. Hell, she doesn't even have clothes on!"

"Wait. What?" Even Doug seemed flustered at that.

"It must have been a really bad situation. She bailed in the middle of the night with nothing but an old, baggy T-shirt. What should I do?" Austin lifted his hands, feeling kind of helpless. "Give her money? Call the cops? See if there's some kind of shelter nearby?"

"What's your gut telling you?" asked James, always impulsive.

Austin hesitated. Should he admit it? Fuck it, yes. That's why he'd called them. They understood and shared his instincts. "That I should take her home with me until she can figure things out."

To his surprise, Bryant didn't immediately object. "Would she take off with a stranger considering even someone she might have trusted did wrong by her?"

"I don't know." Austin considered how she'd fought him. "Probably not. She doesn't have many options, though. How can I convince her it's okay? That I'm not like the asshole that hurt her or someone trying to take advantage of the circumstances?"

"You're decent with the difficult animals on the ranch," Doug said. "My dad always hoped you'd join him on the horse breeding side of things."

He had? Huh. Austin hadn't realized his uncle had thought that highly of his help around the equestrian operation.

Maybe he should get more involved during his stints at the ranch.

Bryant seconded Doug's faith. "Yeah. Do what you do with the horses. Be gentle. Patient. Listen to her and alleviate any of her concerns. I bet she'll go with you, at least until you find somewhere safe."

James laughed. "You know, what they're really saying is, 'Do exactly the opposite of what you usually do with women.' Don't go alpha cowboy on her ass. Dial down the intensity a notch or two. And keep your damn tattoos covered so you look less like a freak and more...well, like Bryant."

That's the pot calling the kettle black, Austin thought. James was every bit as alpha as he was, which was why they sometimes butted heads.

Bryant shot their cousin the finger. He might be the scholar among them, but he would still resort to a brawl if James kept insulting him.

"Uh, I can try," Austin mumbled. Did he really act that way? Yeah, kind of. Oops.

Maybe he'd been out here on the road a little too long. He'd started to see women in terms of a one-night affair. There wasn't time to waste on pleasantries when he was pulling out at first light.

A change could be good for him.

"Whatever you do, be careful. Please," Bryant urged. "Don't do anything crazy."

Right then the waitress set two to-go boxes on Austin's table along with his change.

"Okay, then I'd better go. Because she's locked inside my truck." He waited for his cousins to work it out.

Doug cracked up. James snorted. A muscle twitched in Bryant's jaw. "Meaning you gave her your keys? You idiot. Go!"

"Have fun!" James shouted over Bryant's outrage.

"Call us tomorrow and let us know what happened," Doug demanded. "In detail!"

With a wave and a grin, Austin signed off, determined to earn his stowaway's trust.

Damn, he missed those guys.

7

———————

Hayden couldn't believe this was happening. She'd finally stopped shivering long enough for her entire body to go slack. She lay in a stranger's bed, staring up at the ceiling of his tidy and extremely cozy tractor-trailer, somehow more relaxed than she'd been in her own home for longer than she cared to admit.

Though she hadn't entirely ruled out the possibility that he could be a serial killer or rapist luring her into a trap, his thoughtfulness in giving her some solitude and sanctuary went a long way toward reassuring her about his good intentions. His willingness to trust her—someone who'd just attempted to rob him—either made him dumb or unbelievably compassionate. The intensity of his stare and his quick wit ruled out stupidity.

Maybe karma was paying her back for putting up with Bobby Joe's shit entirely too long.

She rubbed her growling stomach, which wasn't the only part of her hoping her knight in a red truck would return soon. In his space, she already felt safer. That was sad, she knew, seeing as she'd lived with her ex for more than five years and rightfully had been wary of him.

Hayden snuggled into the handsome stranger's pillow and drew his covers to her chin, pretending she did it for additional heat when really it was all about comfort and security. Her aching bones appreciated the surprisingly lush foam mattress of his bunk. It felt like a cloud compared to the metal floor of the livestock trailer.

When she had another decision to make, she'd consider the next step. For a moment or two, she was content to enjoy the respite from her worries.

She must have faded out for a few minutes or more.

A triple knock on the window startled her. Hayden sat up, clutching a colorful handmade quilt to her chest until she recalled where she was.

"Delivery. One delicious burger and a mountain of fries. I might even have a slice of pie for dessert."

The truck's owner!

Whipping the quilt from the bed, Hayden wrapped it around herself just below her collarbones. She adjusted the borrowed leather jacket on top of it as if it were a matching cardigan to her impromptu strapless dress. Then she shuffled to the front of the cab, squeezed between the seats and stared at her unlikely savior through the window.

"Roll it down if you want me to pass this through so you can eat by yourself." He held up a cardboard box. Steam curled from the sides.

Her mouth actually watered. The pang in her stomach grew to a full on stab in her side. Damn, she needed to eat.

Instead of cracking the window, she impulsively lifted the handle and nudged the door open. It felt absurd to invite him into his own space so she simply stood there instead. Staring at him while he did the same to her.

"You sure?" He hesitated.

She nodded, then retreated to the only spot available. Hayden perched on the edge of his bed.

He boosted himself inside gracefully and handed her the carton before reaching below the passenger seat for a lever that spun the chair around backwards. Sitting, he faced her, giving her as much room as possible in the intimate area. Even still, his legs sprawled dangerously close to hers.

The man was big. Everywhere. He folded his hands in his lap as if to occupy them. She bet he didn't often keep them to himself when he had a woman in here with him. His cowboy boots dwarfed her bare feet, so she drew them beneath the quilt, sitting cross-legged instead.

"Thank you," she murmured. "I don't have any money."

She looked at the floorboards then, hoping he didn't expect some other form of payment for his kindness.

"I didn't expect you to give me cash or anything else." He blew out a huge breath as if trying not to be offended. She hadn't meant to insult him or test his seemingly infinite patience. "Just eat. Please. You must be starving."

Hayden nodded. She didn't have even a single fuck left to give about him watching her devour the massive helping of food like she ordinarily might. Instead, she dug in and showed him exactly how grateful she was for his generosity by plowing through half the burger and most of the fries before looking up from her dinner.

"Better?" he asked softly when she took a break from stuffing her face.

It felt so good to give the churning acid in her stomach something other than her own flesh to devour. Finally, the pang beneath her ribs relented some. It helped her relax further since she'd been trying not to freak out over the thought that some of her discomfort might stem from cracked bones, or worse, caused by Bobby Joe's knee.

She nodded, her mouth too full to reply.

"I'm Austin Compton. I own this truck and drive it for my family's ranch, making deliveries to farms like the one you found me at this morning. Or the slaughterhouse, so people can enjoy fine burgers at roadside diners."

Fortunately, she didn't have any regrets about being a carnivore. She wiped her mouth with a napkin he handed her as she swallowed another big bite, silently thanking the animal who had been sacrificed for her nourishment.

"I'm Hayden." She didn't supply a last name or anything else for that matter.

He had to realize that was no accident. When he didn't hound her for more information, a knot in her lower back loosened. Too much more of this and she would melt into the bed. How could he be so understanding?

She wasn't sure she would be if the situation were reversed.

"Well, Hayden..." He tested her name slowly. It rolled sweetly off his tongue. "How do you feel about lemon meringue pie?"

A groan slipped from between her cracked lips before she could stop it.

"Would you mind splitting it with me? It was the last piece."

"You eat it. This is a lot for me." She had already taken more than she felt comfortable with.

He smiled. "I have a feeling I'm going to enjoy watching you eat it as much as tasting it myself."

"Is that why you're doing this? Do you get off on helping people or something?" she wondered honestly, if kind of rudely.

"Not usually." He shrugged. "Just doing what seems right in the moment. I tend to live that way."

Since that's exactly what she'd committed to doing with her one-step-at-a-time plan, she couldn't argue. When he held the box with the pie out between them and took two forks from his pocket, she was surprised to find that she'd already eaten the last of her main meal.

Dessert sounded better than ever.

Hayden leaned forward and accepted one of the utensils. Neither of them spoke while they alternated digging in and scooping out some of the decadent treat. When she couldn't jam another morsel down her throat, she cried mercy.

Austin polished off the last of the pie in two sumo-sized bites. Then he sat back with a hum and splayed his hands over his flat abdomen. She tried not to notice how his shirt clung to the solid muscles beneath it. No use.

At least she didn't have to feel guilty about it since she was, for the first time in forever, single.

For a while, they sat in comfortable silence, each of them content to soak in the post-meal satisfaction. Hayden tried not to think about what it might be like to share calm and quiet with a man on a permanent basis. It had been so long, if ever, since she'd had the luxury of peace with Bobby Joe.

Tranquility washed through her. Something in her chest unclenched. The shift in pressure inside her allowed the food to settle into her stomach fully. Which was good. Until it was bad.

She gasped as a white-hot pain stabbed her in the side. Not now! Not again!

"Breathe." Austin was there, crouching beside her. His features pinched as he took in the way she clutched her ribs. He laid his hand on her forearm lightly. "Are you okay?"

"Will be." She grimaced. "Must have eaten too fast. Probably too much grease on an empty stomach. It happens to me sometimes."

More and more often lately, she added to herself.

"Are you sure you don't want me to take you to the emergency room or find an urgent care somewhere?" He raked his stare from where she hugged her own chest to the marks on the rest of her body. His face grew grim, losing some of the reassuring composure she'd fed off of more than the food.

Right then she hated Bobby Joe just a little bit more.

"Positive. Probably should have quit before the pie." She rubbed her sternum with a downward pressure in an attempt to combat the acid reflux beginning to sear her from the inside.

Truthfully, it had been worth the discomfort.

"It's a hazard of living on the road." Austin chuckled, then stood to rummage through a storage bin against the side wall of the sleeper cab. After finding what he was looking for, he tossed a bottle to her.

Antacids. Hayden popped the top without second-guessing his endless charity. She chomped down a small handful regardless of how many the directions would have recommended.

"I've got a few other first aid supplies in here. Over-the-counter painkillers, too. You're welcome to take a look or, if you'd prefer, I could clean out a few of those cuts for you." He held up his hands, palms out, as if afraid of overstepping.

It might have been weak of her, but the thought of someone taking care of her was almost as medicinal as whatever he might have tucked away in his provisions.

Hayden swallowed and closed her eyes for a moment. "Would you, please?"

Besides, the last thing she needed was a nasty infection. Though he'd cleaned the trailer, she'd still had open wounds pressed against surfaces that had recently had cows and their poop all over it. Parts of her were already hot and tight. Throbbing. She might have attributed that effect in part to Austin's commanding presence if they hadn't also been painful to the touch.

"Of course," he answered quietly as he gathered alcohol, some gauze, and what looked like antibiotic cream.

Austin carried them to the bed and piled them beside her. He knelt at her feet as he parted the quilt and worked from her toes upward. The first contact of an alcohol wipe against her cuts had her hissing.

"Sorry," he murmured, then rubbed soothing ointment over the spot before taping some gauze over it.

"Takes my mind off my stomachache." She tried to smile, though it probably ended up as more of a grimace when he moved to the next, deeper scrape.

He distracted her from the inadvertent discomfort his tender touches brought her with a constant ramble from then on. His deep, soothing voice lulled her even as he tended to her wounds. "I'm kind of an expert in skinned knees and stuff like this. I have a whole slew of nieces and nephews back home. Well, some of them are really my second cousins, but none of us really make that distinction. I've got one sister and three older girl cousins, plus three boy cousins around my own age. The girls have all settled down in cute cabins on our farm and started families of their own. Plus a bunch of the ranch hands bring their children to work. We've got our own informal daycare running these days. In a place like that, where kids still play outside—like I did growing up—there are bound to be a few scrapes and bruises."

Hayden could hardly imagine somewhere like he described. "It sounds so nice. Like something out of a black-and-white movie."

He grinned as he skipped from the hem of her shirt to the parts of her arms exposed beneath her sleeves without nudging the fabric upward in either area. "Kind of, yeah. My parents live in a house there too. It's definitely where I belong."

The joy etched into his face transformed him, making the strong lines of his face better match the man who'd been nothing short of incredible to her. It immediately became her goal to make him smile more. Even if it made her a little vulnerable to be honest. He deserved to know how much his decency had impacted her.

"Can I apologize in advance for this?" she asked.

"Uh...sure." He tipped his head, peering up at her from

beneath the brim of his hat before taping the last bandage in place.

"You're a lot nicer than you look."

Thankfully, he chuckled. The rich sound bounced around the cab, making it even homier. "Don't let word get out, you'll ruin my reputation."

"Seriously, when I saw you at that first rest area this morning I was terrified of what you'd do if you found me." She shivered remembering how it had paralyzed her into staying in the trailer all day.

"Well, shit. I've never regretted all these tattoos before."

"It's not that. I have one myself. Love them, actually." She hesitated. "It was all of you. Your size, power, and the determination in how you carry yourself. It all screams that you're not someone to fuck with."

"I'm not," he said, deadpan. "I also reserve my ass-kicking abilities for those who deserve them. Like anyone who would dare to threaten or hurt a woman."

She swallowed hard. With him, she'd be safe even if Bobby Joe somehow caught up to her. Too bad she couldn't continue to impose on him.

Just as she prepared herself to thank him profusely then take her leave, he spoke up. "You'd better get some sleep."

Austin threw away the wrappers from the gauze. He tucked the tape and alcohol into their assigned places. Then he shook out a few aspirin before handing them to her along with an unopened bottle of water. Next thing she knew, he was climbing out of the truck.

"Where are you going?"

"Out back. My camping gear is stowed in the locker under the cab. I'll be a lot more comfortable in the trailer than you were last night. You can use my bed." He snapped his teeth together as if he'd like to add some smartass comment, but refrained for her benefit.

She sort of wished he hadn't. It was crazy to think a man like him might find her even a tiny bit desirable, especially given her current state and the situation, but it would have been kind of sweet to hear him let the innuendo fly instead of resorting to his politeness.

"I couldn't..." She shifted, scooting toward the edge of the mattress with some difficulty. When had she gotten so snug in his bed? "You have to drive again tomorrow. Do your job. It wasn't so bad last night. Honestly, I hardly remember it. It would be more than I could have wished for if you'd lend me your sleeping bag—"

"No way. I wasn't raised like that." He took another step down, his boot heel thunking on the pavement.

"Your parents must be amazing." Because of them, she could survive another eight hours on her own. Otherwise, she'd probably have gone crawling home by now. Or frozen or starved to death in the woods. Every minute longer she made it gave her hope she could last a few more.

"They are. All three of them."

Hayden blinked. Huh? The stress of the day and her relief at how things had turned out were making her crash. Hard. "Three parents? Stepmom or stepdad?"

"Neither. It's a long story. Stick around and maybe I'll tell you about it over breakfast." He hesitated. "Better yet, ride with me back to Compass Ranch and I'll introduce you to them."

She snickered at that. Yeah, right. Like he would cart her off to his beloved home. It was a fun thought, though. Something to take her mind off what would really happen when they parted ways in the morning and she was, once again, on her own with nothing.

Austin didn't take his joke any further. Instead, he tipped his hat. "Goodnight, Hayden. Tomorrow's going to be better, I promise."

"You're right. Things are already looking up. Besides, it

couldn't be much worse." She acted without thinking, standing and crossing the few steps until she came face to face with him. Though he was at least a foot taller than her, she had the advantage while she was in the cab. He stood perfectly still, allowing her to bend down to him, making no move to close the gap between them or to increase it either.

Hayden leaned forward and kissed him on the cheek. "Thank you for everything. Seriously. You have no idea what this means to me. You've restored my faith in men."

"Not every guy is a shithead like your ex."

She nodded, her eyes stinging.

"Now get to bed. If you need to use the facilities in the truck stop during the night or anything else, wake me up. I'll go with you. Unless you prefer the rest of the hay, of course."

Hayden clapped her hand over her mouth to contain her unladylike snort.

"Night."

"Sweet dreams," she whispered.

Just before she shut and locked the door, she thought she heard him whisper, "*That's* not going to be a problem, honey."

Hayden grinned as she tucked herself into Austin's bunk and snuggled down for the night.

8

Austin had risen early. By a farm boy's standards, that was saying something. Partly because it wasn't all that comfortable bunking in the trailer, even with the benefit of the top-end gear Hayden hadn't had during her sleepover. Also because he was afraid she might slip away during the night.

Sure enough, at the ass-crack of dawn the door of his truck cracked open, spilling light onto the pavement. He waited until Hayden had clambered out, wincing as her torn-up feet hit the asphalt. He remembered the angry black-raspberry-jam color of them as he'd tended to them the night before and how hard he'd had to clench his jaw to keep from cursing her ex.

That would only have frightened her. She'd needed him to be stronger than that just then. So he'd ignored his own rage, even if it meant he'd kicked the crap out of the bale of hay in the trailer and vented to his cousins afterward.

"Good morning." His voice rumbled and sputtered like a broken-down engine because he'd forsaken coffee while he waited for her to rouse. Yeah, that was it. Or maybe it had more to do with how tragically beautiful she looked attempting to take on the world with next to nothing. Her determination to survive inspired him. Hell, he'd struggled even with advantages and support she clearly didn't have.

Hayden gasped and splayed her hand over her chest as if to keep her heart inside it.

"Sorry. Didn't mean to scare you."

"Do you always sit in the shadows like a mountain lion waiting for a rabbit to hop past?"

"Nah, but I *am* a decent hunter." He grinned, thinking of his pseudo-grandfather. "There's this guy, Jake, who works on our ranch. Been there the longest of anyone, really. He spent a lot of time out in the wilderness on his days off. When he was young, he fell in love with a Native American woman and became obsessed with a lot of her traditions and culture. Especially decades later, after he found out he'd had a son with her. Anyway, he taught me the benefits of waiting quietly and showed me what I might catch with some patience."

Yeah, like a gorgeous girl who needed help she wasn't likely to accept easily.

"I could listen to stories about Compass Ranch all day." She pointed to the wrap on the tractor. "You guys should have your own show or something."

"My mom has a collection of letters she wrote to my father daily when he was working in oil fields in Alaska for like ten years or something. My sister keeps telling her to turn them into a book, but she doesn't think anyone would really be interested in reading them." Austin thought maybe he'd join forces with Hope next time she brought the subject up.

"I would." Hayden leaned against the truck as she eyed the woods behind Austin. Tiny creases wrinkled her brow. Could she be dreading leaving?

"Why don't you hang around just a little longer? I'll grab us some breakfast and tell you all about Jake or anything else you'd like to hear." He tried not to sound like he gave a shit either way. Austin had listened to his parents' tales, too. He'd definitely inherited more than his supposed good looks from his dads and his uncles. "At least then you'll have something warm in your stomach before you set off."

Hayden nibbled her lip as she considered his offer. Somehow he figured it was curiosity more than survival instincts that had her hesitating. "You'll tell me about your parents, like you promised?"

He nodded. "Sure."

She sighed. He couldn't quite tell if it was in relief or exasperation, but he'd take either one as a win. So long as she stayed with him. Finally, she nodded. "A little while longer."

"Eggs, hash browns, and bacon okay?"

She groaned and pressed her stomach. "Yeah. Do me a favor and hold the orange juice, please? It's one of my favorites and will tempt me too much. I'd rather not have another episode like last night. Especially once I'm on my own."

Damn. That had looked like it hurt, too. Considering how she'd hardly flinched at his contact with the rest of her injuries, she probably needed to see a doctor about that. Austin's sister, Hope, was a nurse. Maybe she could help if he could somehow get in touch with her. Or better yet, if he could wrangle Hayden into coming to Compass Ranch.

That was going to take a whole lot of convincing and a shit ton of little-while-longers.

Austin started devising a plan to make it happen.

9

———

Hayden balled up her napkin and tossed it into her empty to-go box. She'd toyed with the last several bites of potatoes for so long, Austin had wondered if she planned to eat them. Maybe she had been hoping—as he had been—that if she never did, she wouldn't have to leave.

Then again, she could have been simply waiting for him to finish telling her how his mom, his father, and his dad had gotten together and made their three-way partnership work.

"That's remarkable. That they were able to overcome so much then stay together all this time despite the odds." She slumped in the passenger seat. "I thought I could do that, too. With Bobby Joe, I mean. Turns out I was wrong. I couldn't keep us together."

"Congratulations on failing. It's not a bad thing if he treated you like that." Austin reached out slowly and brushed his fingers over the bruises peeking from beneath her tattered sleeve.

She groaned, more from embarrassment than physical discomfort, he assumed. "I know it's no excuse, but he never did

63

this before. Got so rough with me, I mean. And I'm pretty sure he was too drunk to know he'd done most of it."

Austin gritted his teeth and silently counted to three to keep from pointing out that someone didn't accidentally punch another person in the face and give them a black eye. "Whatever. I can already tell you weren't the problem."

"I was planning to leave him. I just didn't get out in time." She lifted her gaze to his then, her stare blasting him with the grit he found so damn attractive in her. "He won't ever have the chance to do that to me again."

He believed her. Especially because now he had a name. He knew who the guy was and where he lived, or pretty close to it. Austin planned to ask Uncle Sawyer, Compton Pass's sheriff, to look into the matter. None of the Compass men tolerated brutality.

So he simply nodded and hummed a vague agreement.

"Anyway, what I was trying to say is that I can't even imagine how hard it must be to juggle three sets of priorities and challenges. Two was hard enough."

"I've learned a lot from them about how to make a relationship work." Austin barked out a humorless laugh at his own pathetic track record. "Or at least I think I have. I guess I'd have to have an actual girlfriend to test that theory. It'd be hard not to get a few things right, at least, with so many great role models around."

"Your parents? And Jake, right?" She didn't react to his declaration of his single status.

"Them too." Austin nodded and tried not to smirk as he baited her a bit. "Plus my aunts and uncles and my older sister —who also has two husbands, by the way—and the trio of girl cousins I mentioned yesterday."

Hayden smiled wryly. "Too bad you don't have time to tell me about all of them, too."

Perfect. Austin wished for the same thing. More time to spend showing her that not everyone was like the people she'd known before. How had she been raised to make lasting love and companionship seem so alien to her?

He couldn't imagine doubting it was possible even if he hadn't been lucky enough to find his own counterpart...*yet.* Something in him had always felt he would someday. After all, nearly everyone else he knew had.

What if he didn't? He wasn't getting any younger out here on the road, where it was nearly impossible to find a woman for more than a single night of fun. Well, shit. The instant he hesitated, thinking about it, was all it took to break the spell he'd been trying to cast over Hayden.

Son of a bitch! He needed a little while longer with her.

"Thanks again. For everything." She placed her garbage in the plastic bag he had tied to the cabinet handle. "I guess I need to let you go. I'm sure if it wasn't for me holding you up, you would have been on the road an hour or two ago."

Like he had been the day before. She didn't say it. Didn't have to remind him of the harrowing ride he'd unintentionally given her.

She stood and shuffled toward the door before unwrapping his quilt from around her slender torso. He'd liked the way the colorful fabric had looked hugging her.

"Wait." He couldn't watch her limp away, chin up, without at least trying something. "Would you accept a lift somewhere? You know, the traditional kind. Stay a while in here? With me? I'll tell you about my dad's three brothers and how everyone in town thinks it's hysterical they each had a firstborn daughter to torture them. Especially once they started dating."

Hayden paused. Still, she eyed the trailer like it might be preferable to nearly freeze to death rather than sit next to him. It could have been that she was worried that there was no way out other than bailing onto the shoulder of the highway from a truck traveling at high speeds. He tried not to take it personally.

Austin didn't hound her, sure that if he did, she would vanish.

"You're not making this up, are you?" she asked.

"Don't believe me? Come see for yourself."

She rolled her eyes as if he hadn't extended a legitimate invitation. Despite the urge to correct her, he let the suggestion hang in the air between them. Waiting for her answer was tough for someone used to taking the lead and getting his way. Compton men usually did. Especially with women.

Austin drew on his lessons in patience from Jake, certain they'd never been as important as they were right then. Eventually, she nodded. Compared to his bigger offer of visiting his ranch, a ride didn't seem like so much, he supposed. Hayden asked, "Where are you headed? Another state or two farther away couldn't hurt."

"Compass Ranch is in Compton Pass, Wyoming." He jerked his jaw west. "About six hundred more miles that way."

"Sounds as good a direction as any." Hayden plopped into the seat and buckled her belt. "Let's go. I've never been a navigator before."

"Fortunately, it's a job you can do without pants." He took a chance teasing her just a bit.

Thankfully, she snorted.

Austin started the truck's engine, loving the roar it issued as it came to life. Then he pulled onto the highway as he said, "I'd lend you my sweats but they'd probably look more ridiculous than that skirt you rigged out of my Grandma Vicky's quilt."

"Oh God. She hand-made this for you? Don't tell her. She'll be so pissed." Hayden began to shimmy out of the material.

"Hey, don't." Austin swallowed hard. "She passed away when I was fourteen. I highly doubt she'll wake from the dead to scold us about it. Besides, she was one of the most caring people and generous women ever. She'd be happy you wrapped yourself up in it."

He'd never been jealous of a damn blanket before. Putting his arms around her, sheltering her, and giving her a sense of security would have been even sweeter than the pie they'd shared the night before.

"But it's a family heirloom." She ran her fingers over the seams of an intricate block, admiring it anew.

"Trust me, Vivi would had loved knowing it gave you comfort—and covered your bare ass when you didn't even have clothes." He didn't have to lie about that.

"I'm sorry about your grandmother." Hayden sighed. "She sounds lovely."

"She was. And don't be. She lived a long, full life. Loved completely. Her husband, her children, her family, and her friends. If I manage all that before I croak, I'll consider myself lucky."

"I never knew any of my grandparents."

"Sucks. My grandfather died before I was born. People talk about JD so much, though, I feel like I know him pretty well."

"Must be nice." Her tone held no hints of sarcasm either. "My father raised me. My mom left him shortly after I was born. Not really into the whole parent lifestyle, I guess. He was so bitter about it, he kept me away from her side of the family. His own parents had disconnected from him because they didn't approve of my mom in the first place. The only times he reached out to them when I was a child, I remember there being a lot of we-told-you-so and shouting. Needless to say, we didn't stick around for that."

"Why didn't he get you out of the situation with your ex?" Austin tried not to judge a man he'd never met. It was tough.

"We don't speak." Hayden cleared her throat. "My fault,

mostly. I'm stubborn. Definitely his daughter. He remarried when I was a senior in high school. Moved out of state with his new wife. I refused to leave Bobby Joe. Told my dad he was jaded when he insisted young love couldn't last and that Bobby Joe wasn't the guy I thought he was."

She buried her face in her hands then.

"Hey, just because it didn't work out doesn't mean it couldn't have." Austin felt it necessary to defend her. "Seems to me like a grown man shouldn't be so immature when it comes to his only child. I've fucked up plenty of times. My parents are always there to help me get my shit back together when I do. It's sort of their job, isn't it?"

She shrugged. "I have no idea what Dad thinks about the situation. He never contacted me again after our humungous fight, when he drove off to his new life. It surprised me, to be honest. That he held a grudge so long considering his parents had essentially done the same thing to him. I tried to reach out about six months after that. His cell number had changed and my email to him bounced. It pissed me off, and crushed me. So I didn't try again. But I don't have a lot of options now. Whenever I get to where I'm going, I'll have to look him up. Hopefully he'll be happy to see me after all this time."

"I'm sure he will be, Hayden." Austin lifted his hand from the gear shift and held it out, palm up, in her direction. He wasn't sure she would take it. "Blood is thicker than water, right?"

When she entwined her fingers with his, something inside him relaxed for the first time since she'd agreed to come along after breakfast. She said, "Did you know that quote doesn't mean what most people think it means?"

"Um, no. I'm not very smart. Dropped out of college." After he'd broken the news to his parents—who had seemed completely unsurprised by his decision—he'd never really been ashamed of it either. He worked his ass off and made a meaningful contribution to his family. That was good enough for him.

"Really?" She squinted at him, then shrugged. "Well, I never went to college at all. But yeah, some people believe the original saying was, 'The blood of the covenant is thicker than the water of the womb.' Meaning people you fight alongside become closer than relatives."

"How do you know that?" he wondered. To him it made better sense. Sure, he had a fierce bond with the rest of the Compton clan, but that included people like Jake and his aunts, who'd become integral members of their family despite being born outside of it.

"I like to read, and the library is free. Can't say that about most other entertainment."

"Well, hopefully your dad isn't a bookworm."

One corner of her lips kicked up, making his grip on the wheel tighten. With his other hand, he brushed his thumb across her knuckles. Damn, she was pretty, even when broken.

"Unfortunately, I inherited that from him, too." She sighed.

On that somber note, their conversation trailed off.

Austin paid careful attention to the road. That didn't keep him from noticing in his peripheral vision that Hayden observed him instead of the scenery flying past mile after mile. It shocked him since studying the earth, watching it roll beneath his tires, and finding his place in it had been one of his favorite pastimes for years now. He felt grounded, part of the dirt. Being out here, surrounded by it, always soothed him.

Could he do that for her? He hoped so.

Their silence didn't last forever. He eventually needed to reclaim his hand to shift and steer. When he did, she started peppering him with questions about the ranch and his family. They talked and laughed for hours. It was easy to share things with her, both the good and the bad. The sentimental stuff along with the wacky antics of his relatives. Hell, she knew better than most that the road winding through life climbed over mountains and plunged into valleys.

Who knew what was around the next turn?

Eventually, he approached a trucker's outpost on the most barren stretch of their route. It consisted of a gas station, a few shitty fast food joints, and a mega-mart isolated from civilization for hundreds of miles in every direction.

Ideal for what he had in mind.

He put on his blinker then downshifted as he took the next exit.

"Do you need gas?" Hayden tried to peek at his gauges as he eased the semi into the outer lot of the big-box store. She fidgeted as she glanced out the window at a whole lot of nothing.

"Yeah." But not as much as he needed to take the next step in his plan. "And I have to grab a couple of things from here."

Austin parked, then stretched. Hayden kept craning her neck without luck. He could have told her there wasn't much around. Which was exactly why he'd picked the place. She didn't have a lot of options there.

"I guess this is my stop then." She pasted on a brave smile anyway.

"You've hung out with me all morning, why not stay a while longer? I'll run in and grab you some clothes so at least when we make it to someplace less remote you can be on your way. You'll blend in better, be able to ask around for work, and won't freeze your ass off in the meantime."

Her mouth opened. Then closed. Then opened again.

Still no argument came forth. Hayden nodded.

"Smart choice." He sealed the deal with one parting shot as he hopped out of the cab. It wasn't a line. It was one-hundred percent truth. "Besides, it's nice to have someone along for the ride. The road gets lonely sometimes."

Even Austin wasn't sure if he meant the highway, or his path through life. He'd have plenty to talk about with his cousins next time they got together, in person or virtually.

Hayden visibly relaxed, melting into her seat.

"I'll be right back," he promised, then set off at a jog.

If she vanished before he returned, he didn't know what he would do.

10

———

Hayden wrinkled her nose as she squinted at Austin, who marched toward the truck. He towed a suitcase behind him. She might have figured he'd needed it himself if it hadn't been holographic pink. Not exactly his style, she guessed, as she took in how it clashed with his ripped jeans, boots, and cowboy hat.

What had he done?

Her heart galloped as wildly as the horses he'd told her about, which waited for him in an idyllic pasture back home. She'd already taken far more from him than she should have. Gotten too comfortable with a stranger. Was it because of how fucking scared she was? Their jaunt was only delaying the inevitable. Soon enough she'd truly be out on her own in the world.

Every minute she spent with Austin made that thought as terrifying as it had been while she prepared to leave Bobby Joe. She had to do this. Stand by herself. At the next halfway decent town they passed through, she'd ask him to let her out.

Her chest tightened, squeezing painfully and making it tough to breathe properly.

Austin's long legs erased the distance between them before she could do more than rub the ache between her breasts. He opened his door, hefted the suitcase inside, then stepped up behind it. His grin combated some of the toughness his tattoos lent him. It made him seem younger, much closer to her own age.

Was he that glad to see her? Had he expected her to vanish?

If they'd been somewhere she could have set down roots, she probably would have. Now that he'd returned, it was hard to remember why it was important for her to establish her independence when it was so much easier to stay sheltered under his wing.

"Were they out of plastic bags?" she asked with an arched brow. Hopefully she didn't seem ungrateful. It was just that he was going so far above and beyond that she felt like she was starting to take advantage of his kindness.

Definitely leaving at the next stop, she swore to herself.

He chuckled. "Nah, I figured you'd need at least enough stuff to make it through the next week or two until you can find your dad. This seemed easier. Just pretend you're on vacation or something."

She'd never gone on that sort of trip, purely for the fun of it. However, it did seem like she'd taken a major detour from her old life, so she might as well enjoy the scenery on this road they were briefly traveling together. Especially since it included a sexy cowboy trucker with an enormous...heart. His devotion to his family and his concern for a complete stranger told her everything she needed to know about his capacity to love.

"Go ahead. Open it. If there's anything I didn't think of, I expect you to say so." He stuffed one hand in the pocket of his jeans as he nudged the suitcase toward her with his knee. Then he got behind the wheel and said, "I'm going to fuel us up while you see how good of a personal shopper I'd make if this truck-driving shit doesn't pan out."

Though he was obviously joking, she realized she'd delayed him yet again.

"I'm sorry I cost you more time." She hesitated, biting her lip.

"Don't be. Nobody's expecting me on a particular schedule. I mean, sometimes I take the long way home when I've got an empty trailer like this. See the world a bit. Meet new people." The way he adjusted himself in the seat without looking at her when he said that last part made her sure that was secret code for sometimes-I-shack-up-with-women-I-meet-on-the-road. A man as generous and compassionate as him could probably devastate any woman he took to bed.

Maybe if they'd met under different circumstances…

She shook her head to clear that bit of wishful thinking when he said, "You're not going to get all stubborn about this, are you? My sister warned me you might—"

"You talked to Hope about me?" She tilted her head. "When?"

"Oh. Uh. Yeah. She called while I was in the store." He shrugged. "I didn't think you would mind since I pretty much told you her life story."

"I don't except that I'm pathetic compared to her." Hayden wished she could afford to decline his help. "And no, I'm not. Going to dig in my heels, I mean. This is a huge help. Seriously, thank you. Again."

"Don't mention it." When the truck rumbled to life, he guided it to the gas station. She might have sat there and admired the flex of his inked arm muscles or his striking profile some more—as she had for hundreds of miles—except when she unzipped the lid of the suitcase and flipped it open, she gasped.

Austin hadn't only bought her clothes, though there were several pairs of jeans and a selection of soft, pretty tops that she could mix and match into any number of outfits. He'd also tossed in a couple packs of socks and underwear, a pair of sneakers, and a light jacket. He must have a lot of experience or had checked her out more closely than she realized because he'd nailed everything, right down to her bra size.

She rummaged through the mesh pocket on the inside of the lid. A toothbrush, deodorant, a comb, soap, shampoo, and some first aid supplies like he'd used on her the night before rounded out his picks. The fresh baby powder scent of the toiletries made her realize she probably didn't smell anywhere near as good as they did.

"Are you telling me I need a shower?" She sniffed her pits, figuring he was probably right.

"What? No!" His face blanched. "I spend most of my days around cow shit. You can't possibly stink as much as that."

Hayden cracked up at his brutal honesty. She'd take that. "A low bar, but...okay."

He wiped his hand across his brow as if relieved she wasn't pissed as he parked the truck near the fuel pump.

"I really do appreciate this, Austin. It's too much." She stepped closer to the driver's seat, bent over, and hugged him. Hayden added a quick peck on the cheek without thinking about it first. If she had, she might have kept her hands and lips to herself. Would he have preferred a more rewarding kiss instead?

Though part of her was curious about how it would feel to make out with someone different after all this time, she was relieved he didn't pressure her or seem to expect anything in return for his assistance.

"It's not a big deal. I'm glad there's something simple I can do to make things easier for you. I'm going to pump the gas. Why don't you try that stuff on and make sure it fits while I'm gone?"

"I sort of like my quilt dress. You're right, though. Real clothes will make it look less like I just busted out of an insane asylum or something." She smiled at him as he mumbled something beneath his breath.

It sounded suspiciously like, "I think you'd look better naked."

"What was that?" she asked, oddly flattered rather than offended.

"Nothing. Be right back." He didn't turn around before shutting the door and leaving her to herself again.

Hayden tore off tags and slipped into the first thing she put her hands on. It felt so freeing to be quasi-normal again. Even better, she discovered the receipt for her new possessions at the bottom of the suitcase.

She winced. It would take a while to pay Austin back, though the total wasn't too bad considering it was the price of everything she owned in the entire world. Flipping the receipt over, she returned to what she now thought of as her seat, dropping into it cross-legged. Then she nabbed a pen from the dash and started making notes on the back.

The total from the receipt went at the top. Next she listed everything Austin had paid for her. Dinner, breakfast, gas... Then she rounded up a bit. She wrote *interest* next to that figure but in her mind she thought of it as a bonus for being an awesome man.

Austin rejoined her about the time she finished tallying everything. She drew a circle around the total as he leaned over to see what she was doing. "What the hell is that?"

"My bill." She proudly showed him her calculations.

In a flash, his hand darted out and snatched the paper from her fingers. He'd already started ripping it to bits by the time she could shout, "Don't!"

Hayden lunged toward him. Her hands wrapped around his wrists in an attempt to reclaim the confetti he'd turned her IOU list into. No use. "It's only fair. Please. Let me salvage a shred of my damn pride, would you?"

He froze at that. "Shit, I didn't mean to insult you."

"Whatever. I know where you live. I'll send a check to your mom and tell her to buy you something nice for Christmas." She stopped fighting but left her hands resting lightly on him for a moment more. Hayden squeezed, then forced herself to let go and retreat to her side of the cab.

"You're going to stay a little longer, right?" he asked. "At least until we get to a bigger town. I think we should be somewhere that works better for you around dinnertime."

There really wasn't much opportunity for her here. So she nodded. "That sounds perfect. Who are you going to tell me about next?"

She wasn't stupid. She knew what he was up to. But somewhere a few hundred miles back, she'd stopped caring and allowed herself to enjoy his distractions. Why silence him when she didn't really want to? Why object when she had nowhere else to go anyway?

Austin was right. She needed to end up someplace she could start over. This roadside pit stop wasn't it. She needed some actual civilization. Preferably someplace she could work a few jobs and find a place to stay for a bit. A town with a public library and free internet access would be ideal.

As she deliberated her options, she started humming along with the radio as she often did during her shift cleaning the motel. Music transported her to a place without problems.

"Do you like this song?" Austin asked as he turned it up.

She did. So she sang, softly at first, in case he shushed her as Bobby Joe had always done.

Louder when he beamed at her before pulling the truck back onto the highway.

He added a decent enough harmony to her melody until commercials interrupted their karaoke session. Austin shot her an appreciative glance. "You have a great voice."

"Thanks. You're not too shabby either," she answered reflexively.

"Nothing like you. You remind me of my aunt, Leah." Just like that, he was regaling her with more of his family history. The next several hours passed in a blur, no matter how often she wished she could slow the ticking of time.

All too soon, they were turning into yet another roadside establishment. The lights of a mid-sized city flickered behind the easy access.

This was it.

Her stop.

She drew a deep breath and steeled herself to say goodbye. Before she could find the right words to express her gratitude, Austin took charge.

"Maybe you should stay just a little longer and have dinner with me. This place has decent food and live entertainment. There are shower facilities, too." His voice dropped, both in volume and pitch, as if he was afraid this time she'd decline his invitation.

She didn't have the heart to ruin their running joke. "Hmm, I guess I could grab a bite to eat, clean up, and *then* be on my way."

This time for sure.

Her stomach knotted as she thought of losing her only ally in the world. Acid splashed the persistent soreness inside her guts, making her groan softly. She'd gotten incredibly lucky crossing paths with someone as honorable as him. Someone who appealed to her in a variety of ways. A few of which she chalked up to years locked in a stagnant relationship.

There was no way she could have as much chemistry with him as it felt like, right? It was just his decency that made him seem so much more attractive than Bobby Joe, wasn't it?

Hayden had one last supper to figure it out.

11

———————

The Crispy Biscuit Diner. Austin had been there before. Often. But he'd never enjoyed his company as much as he would tonight. Good thing Regina had the night off. The aggressive lot lizard was also a server here. He'd barely swatted her away on the first leg of this journey, and not before she'd slipped her schedule and phone number to him on a dirty napkin two days ago. He'd promptly balled it up and tossed it in the trash.

Her attempts to seduce him were growing bolder yet no more effective each time he ran into her. She wasn't the kind of woman he enjoyed. The superficial veneer of beauty she relied on to entice lonely men on the road didn't do it for him. Never once had she laughed at his jokes or asked about where he was from or managed to make it through a single dance with him before flirting with other guys and stepping on his toes.

Though the stories he'd heard over the truck's CB radio guaranteed Regina could entertain his body for a night or two, it would be an empty exchange. Something he wasn't finding much satisfaction in lately. At the very least he'd rather enjoy the company of a local who was enthusiastic about getting naked with him because she shared a lusty spark with him, not because she made a living by manufacturing something that wasn't there naturally.

Austin held the door for Hayden, who rocked the jeans and periwinkle sweater he'd bought for her. Her subtle curves called out to his hands, making him wish he could stroke the fuzzy material warmed by the heat of her body. Right before he took those clothes off her.

After she passed, he stealthily adjusted the growing bulge in his pants. Not again. He'd been hard as hell for most of the day, wishing he could soothe Hayden's pain and calm her anxiety in a much more primal fashion. Her stoic fight to survive triggered instincts he hadn't realized he'd inherited from the older generation of Compass men.

It was probably best that she was about to ditch him. It would keep things from becoming awkward. He couldn't hide his hunger for her much longer.

How he'd kept things civil this long, he couldn't say.

Oh right, it probably had something to do with the shiner she'd obscured a little too easily with the cheap makeup Hope had insisted he add to his cart during their emergency shopping videochat. When Hayden had caught his suspicious glower, she'd sworn she had practice because she was used to hiding dark circles after working graveyards at a local motel then taking the breakfast shift at the diner where she'd waited tables.

Hopefully she was telling the truth. Working herself to the point of exhaustion to support a piece-of-shit boyfriend was bad enough. She deserved to have someone look after her for a change.

Austin didn't think before resting his hand on the small of her back and guiding her toward the stools at the bar. It made something animalistic inside him howl in victory when she didn't flinch at his possessive touch. Things were going better than he'd expected. He was two steps away from persuading her to ditch her plan in favor of riding the rest of the way to Compass Ranch with him in the morning. If he didn't fuck up in the next hour or so and then the rest of the night, he might have a shot at convincing her that was her best option.

She smiled over her shoulder at him when she put one foot on the chair rail. He cupped her elbow and steadied her, boosting her into the tall seat beside his usual spot.

When he claimed his place next to her, she leaned toward him and asked, "What's good here?"

Before he could meet her halfway to give his recommendation and soak in the nearness to her, a familiar saccharine voice called out from behind him, "Hey, handsome! Didn't think I'd have the pleasure of your company twice in one week."

Regina sidled up, pressed her side to the bar between Austin and Hayden's stools, then draped her arm along its surface in his direction. The move effectively boxed him in while cutting off his line of sight to Hayden. If he guessed right, Regina might have jostled his temporary co-pilot with her generous ass. That primordial part of him was back, this time baring its teeth in a warning their server seemed oblivious to.

"Hello." If he was civil though curt, maybe she would follow his lead. Hopefully Hayden realized that Regina's false insinuation was nothing more than wishful thinking. Nothing dirty had happened between them earlier in the week. Or ever, for that matter. "Could I get two menus? One for me and another for my guest?"

"Her?" Regina peered over her shoulder as if expecting to see another trucker instead of a pretty young woman she couldn't possibly have missed on her way over. Hayden wasn't the kind of girl who faded into the background. The tip of Regina's pen flicked against her order pad. "Hmmm. You didn't mention you were picking up any heifers on this trip."

"Excuse me?" Hayden bristled and began to rise. "If I'm not welcome—"

"*You* are." Austin deliberately ignored Regina and stared directly at Hayden so she could see for herself that he was dead serious. No fucking way was Regina going to ruin his hard work and patience. Apparently the harmless flirtation he'd engaged in with her in the past hadn't been quite so inconsequential after all. Damn his momma for raising him to pay compliments that could sometimes be misconstrued.

"Hey, Charlie!" Austin shouted to a balding guy who was finishing wiping spots off glasses at the other end of the bar. The Biscuit's owner didn't take shit from anyone. He kept this place running smoothly even when it was full of bored, drunk cowboys and truckers competing for the scarce supply of female attention. A dangerous combination. "Can you seat us in a booth in someone else's section?"

The man swung around. His eyes narrowed as he took in Regina and her obvious violation of Austin and Hayden's personal space. Then he clomped over.

"Damn it, Regina." He wrung his hands on the wet dishtowel. "You know I don't have time for this crap. First Diamond cancelled and left us without an act for tonight, now you're ruining people's appetites. Go home. Come in tomorrow if you can quit pissing off our customers."

She flipped him the bird, whipped her apron off, and spiked it to the floor. Before storming out of the diner, she spat, "You'll be lucky if I come back at all."

"Yeah, yeah. What's this, the third time you've quit this month?" Charlie shook his head and turned to Austin and Hayden. "Sorry about that. She's my wife's bratty little sister. Used to getting her way."

"I bet." Hayden watched until the other woman vanished with an exaggerated swing of her hips. "If your wife resembles her at all, you're a lucky man. She's beautiful and has a lot of... uh...assets."

Austin nearly choked. Then he realized she was serious. "You've got plenty of your own."

Charlie chuckled as he tried to discreetly check Hayden out. Austin didn't blame the guy. It had to be obvious he was about to start drooling, and not over the smell of the daily special either.

Hayden didn't seem to catch the knowing glance the guys exchanged. She surprised Austin when she spun back around and addressed Charlie. "If you need help, I'm willing to work for our dinners and a token for the shower facilities. I have a lot of experience as a waitress or a greeter or even as a dishwasher. Heck, I clean a mean toilet and I..."

She trailed off, making Austin lean forward, wondering what she'd been about to say.

"We're going to have plenty of extra staff if there's no entertainment." Charlie cursed. "Thanks anyway."

"Welcome," Hayden mumbled. Her shoulders slumped. Then the most amazing thing happened. Austin watched as she mustered some grit from the bottom of her battered soul and tried a different tactic. "Actually, if you wouldn't mind lending me that guitar up on stage, I play. I have a halfway decent voice. I think. It's kind of hard to tell for sure since most of the people who clap for me are hammered, but I've never had a tomato thrown at me. I know a lot of country songs. I can take requests. I'd be happy to do a quick audition for you if you'll take the time to listen."

Charlie gawked at her, then said to Austin, "Where'd you find this one?"

"In my livestock trailer." When Charlie blinked a few times in rapid succession, Austin shrugged. "Long story. But I did hear her singing earlier today. She's great. At least as good as your usual lady. You'd be crazy not to take her up on her offer."

"This *is* nuts." Charlie raised his hands then dropped them so they clapped against his sides.

"You're right. Sorry to be so pushy—" The fierceness drained from Hayden's stance.

Austin swore he'd never come back to this shithole again if he was reading the situation wrong. He'd caught a glimpse of the woman Hayden really was beneath the lingering taint of her recent trouble. Enough rejection would eventually smother her fighter's spirit for good.

So he intervened, determined to see that side of her again. To watch it flourish. "Hayden, I think Charlie's wondering how he got so fucking lucky."

Ironically, so was Austin.

He might have helped Hayden out of a bad situation, but spending time with her had showed him it was time to change his course again. Time to quit fooling around and find a companion who could stave off the loneliness creeping in on him lately.

It had taken meeting her to realize how isolated he'd become.

Though she wasn't likely to stick around long enough to do more than awaken desires he'd thought long lost, he'd never forget her for kick-starting his seized heart.

"Is that true?" Hayden tipped her head and peeked from beneath her lashes at Charlie, making her seem like a curious kitten.

The guy laughed out loud. A rich boom Austin had never heard from the overworked bastard echoed around the restaurant. "Hell yes! Thank you for saving my ass."

"Hang on." Austin gripped Charlie's upper arm hard enough to get the man's undivided attention. "What will you pay her?"

"Hey, you're not my pimp. I've got this." Hayden shoved Austin. The force of her palms on his chest rocked him, though she couldn't do any real damage. He loved when she put her hands on him, even if it was to push him away. How sick was that?

"Aim higher. You're worth more than what you've asked for." Fuck if he'd see her fleeced.

Hayden hesitated, then she said to Charlie, "If you could comp our meals and the shower, plus give me a reference in the future, I'd really appreciate that."

Charlie glanced at Austin. The diner's owner might have taken advantage of Hayden's modest requests if Austin hadn't crossed his arms. The heels of his boots thunked on the wooden floor when he widened his stance. Subtly, he shook his head no.

"Of course I'll do that. But I insist you also take a cut of the bar receipts and put out a tip jar, too."

That was more like it.

"I couldn't..." Hayden gasped.

"She'll take it," Austin talked over her.

Even if she was pissed at him for interfering and would no longer need him quite as much with some cash in her pocket, she'd be better off when they finally parted ways. That was most important.

"So what can I get you for dinner?" Charlie asked them.

Austin ordered his usual open-faced roast beef sandwich with a pile of mashed potatoes. When Hayden didn't answer as quickly, Charlie offered to get her a menu. She shook her head. "It's not that. It's probably not a good idea for me to eat before I perform. I'm kind of nervous and I get this thing in my side after I eat when I'm stressed out."

She looked away and Austin frowned. Maybe last night had been something more serious than nearly indigestible greasy highway food.

"How about a bowl of chicken noodle soup and a bunch of crackers now, then whatever you like to go after we shut things down tonight?" Charlie suddenly morphed into some kind of paternal fairy godfather. Just like that, Hayden had wrapped the Biscuit's owner around her pinky.

Hayden nodded but didn't speak. Her throat flexed and her cheeks flushed. Her gorgeous eyes went glassy. Oh fuck. If she broke down, Austin would lose it. A woman's tears had the power to rip him up. And he had a feeling hers would be twice as potent as any other woman's besides his sister's or cousins'.

So he took emergency measures and enfolded her in his arms.

She stiffened in his hold for a moment. Just when he was about to let her go and apologize, she melted against him, resting her cheek on his shoulder.

"You're going to be great," he whispered against her temple. With a feather-light kiss there and a few rubs of his palm across her back, he forced himself to release her.

"Thank you," she murmured as she stared up at him with wide eyes.

When they separated, Austin realized Charlie had already taken off to feed her. Funny, when they'd been wrapped in each other, he hadn't noticed anything happening around them.

His tunnel vision only got stronger throughout the night. How could he take his eyes off Hayden as she moved to the music she made, drawing in the entire crowd with her heartfelt delivery of lyrics and the uniquely modified covers of classics that suited her own chill, coffeehouse style? God, she was fantastic.

As she swayed in time to her strumming, she damn near hypnotized him. And when she sang, it sounded like she was delivering each lyric directly to him. Especially when she switched from an up tempo song to a ballad.

What the fuck was happening here?

He still hadn't figured it out by the time she closed her set to thunderous applause, whistles, and more than a few cat calls from men hoping for a private encore.

Austin shoved his way through the crowd to catch her as she flung herself from the stage into his waiting arms. He confessed, "I was wrong. You were so much better than great."

"You think so?" Her eyes sparkled, this time with joy instead of sadness or fear. It didn't seem possible, but she was even more beautiful than before. Now her dazzling smile nearly split her face, teasing him with the parting of her lush lips. Her hands rested on his shoulders as he lowered her to the floor.

"Absolutely. In fact, I'll be shocked if Charlie doesn't offer you Diamond's job permanently." Though it would suck if she had already reached her final destination, Austin would be glad if that meant she had somewhere decent to stay and someone to look out for her until she got back on her feet.

"Oh, I would never screw somebody over like that." Her enthusiasm dimmed, making him curse himself silently. "I hope he doesn't think..."

"Nah. He's not going to be pissed if you're set on being a one-time act." Austin collected her stuffed tip jar and tucked it into the crook of his arm, content to be her security detail. She grabbed his hand and tugged him toward the kitchen. "Although I have to say I've never seen it this packed in here before. I bet you'll rake it in on the bar receipts."

"Perfect." She squeezed his fingers. "I can put a down payment on what I owe you."

Austin recoiled, jerking her to a stop just outside the kitchen. "What? No."

"You said you'd let me pay you back." Hayden shook her hand out of his grasp and propped it on her hip. "I'm going to do it."

"Easy, tiger." He couldn't help but admire her independent streak since he had one, too. "I don't mean never. I just mean you should build up some funds first. Once you're settled, that's a different story. Okay?"

Though she hesitated, eventually she nodded.

Then she lunged forward and hugged him tight enough the poor tip jar was in danger of exploding. "I can't believe how much my life has changed in less than two days. You have no idea. This is a dream come true."

That something so simple could be everything she asked for humbled him. Like that time he'd dropped out of college, he had some serious thinking to do about his priorities and goals in life soon. Who knew what the outcome would be?

Hayden might not know it, but she'd impacted his life at least as much as he had hers.

Fuck, he wasn't ready to say goodbye. "Why don't you put in your order then take your shower? If you want some peace during supper, you can eat in my truck. We can use my laptop to find a decent place for you to stay and I'll drop you off...if that's what you really want."

"What other choice do I have?" She backed up just enough to meet his stare with her questioning gaze.

Come with me. He thought the words but didn't muster the courage to say them out loud. If he reached too far, too fast now, he could lose her to a kneejerk refusal. "Why don't we talk about it somewhere quieter?"

He was shouting over the recorded music blaring in the background and the guys who kept trying to interrupt to tell her how amazing she was in the hopes of sweet-talking their way into a dance, a few drinks...or more.

Hayden bit her lip then nodded. Was his imagination playing hopeful tricks on him, or did she seem kind of disappointed?

They'd find out soon enough.

12

─────────

"I really can't believe this." Hayden stared at the money mounded on Austin's bunk like she was thinking of cannonballing into it as if it were a pile of autumn leaves instead of crumpled ones, fives, tens, and even a smattering of twenties. "You're sure there's no mistake?"

It had shocked him too, to be honest. Charlie had insisted, though, that he hadn't padded Hayden's take. She'd earned every bit of that cash by keeping the Crispy Biscuit's customers happy and thirsty longer than usual. "Nope. It's all yours."

"Wow." She plopped beside him, lifted a handful then let the bills flutter back to his bed.

Fresh from the shower, her hair seemed even longer than before. It hung nearly to her waist now that the gentle waves were straightened by the weight of the damp strands. With her face washed clean, she looked younger and more innocent, too.

It made him uncomfortable with the naughty thoughts that kept creeping into his mind, seeing her perched there on his bunk.

"Will you count it for me while I eat? I'll get out of your hair soon, I promise."

"No hurry. Don't rush. I don't want you to get sick again." He lowered his voice and looked down at the money as he began to gather and organize it for her. If she was anything like his sister or cousins, she might be offended by what he said next, but he couldn't help himself. "Maybe you should use some of this to see a doctor about that."

"Been meaning to." She nodded. "Too bad I don't have a big sister like Hope. If I did, she could sneak me into her practice on short notice."

"I'm sure she would be willing to try if you'd like me to give her a call." Austin froze, afraid of even breathing wrong. He tried to pretend it was no big deal either way when that's exactly what he'd been aiming for all along.

"Wyoming is kind of far for an appointment when you don't own a car." She smiled as she cracked open her takeout box. She'd opted for a simple grilled chicken breast without seasoning, a scoop of mashed potatoes without any toppings and some steamed vegetables. Bland as shit, he figured.

Come with me. What if she said no? What if she wasn't ready for whatever attraction he could feel swirling around them in the intimate quarters? Eventually one of them would crack. Was it selfish to admit he grew more curious about what she would taste like every moment they spent together?

Given her situation, he figured it was.

"I guess." He let it drop, instead focusing his attention on counting out her take while she inhaled her dinner. Performing for hours must have taken a lot out of her. While engrossed in her music, he never would have guessed the stress she'd been under lately. You could only bury that shit for so long before it drained you.

When she tossed her garbage and leaned against the side of the cab with a sigh, he asked, "Better?"

"Much." Hayden hugged her stomach as her eyelids

drooped. Until she realized he'd separated the money into five neat piles. "Hang on. How much is in each one of those?"

"A hundred. Except that last one, it's a few bucks short."

"Five hundred dollars?" She grabbed one for a recount. "Are you sure?"

"I'm decent at math. Not as good as my cousin Bryant but, you know. Yeah." He chuckled when her jaw went slack.

"This is what I used to make in a week."

"Get used to it. From what I saw tonight, it won't be hard for you to book this kind of gig more often, if that's something you'd be passionate about pursuing."

"Holy shit." She covered her face with her hands. The fine tremble in her fingers got to him. Austin couldn't sit there, unmoved, by her smashing through the roadblocks to her happiness. He scooted closer until they sat side by side, then put his arm around her shoulders. "You absolutely killed it tonight. Congratulations. You deserve every bit of this and more."

Jake's lessons in patience paid off when Hayden turned to him, buried her face against his chest, and placed one palm on his torso to steady herself. He wondered if she could feel his abs clenching in response to her gentle touch.

"Thank you, so much."

"I didn't do it. You did." He dropped a kiss on her temple. "I just cheered."

"You'll never understand how much that means to me," she said quietly before relaxing into his hold. They sat there together, unmoving, for a while. Until she yawned.

"Getting sleepy?" he asked.

"Yeah." Her breasts pressed against his side when she sighed. "Can I use your computer now to look for a place to go?"

"You can, but you don't have to. Why don't you stay a little longer? It's late enough you might as well crash here again and leave at first light. It'll save you a night of hotel fees. Seems silly to waste it since I'm here anyway."

Hayden beamed at him, and the glory of her genuine bliss nearly broke his no-boner mandate. "I was afraid you wouldn't ask."

"Consider it a standing invitation." He brushed her hair back from her temple and tucked it behind her ear. That's when he realized they were drawing toward each other as if pulled by unseen forces. Should he squash the urge, put some distance between them before he crossed a line that would send her running for sure?

No way would she be ready for that. Besides, he didn't want to imply that he expected her to express her gratitude in an inappropriate fashion. He might have been horny, but he wasn't an opportunistic bastard who preyed on women in unfortunate situations.

Instead, he brushed his cheek over her forehead lightly before turning away so she couldn't see how desperately he wanted her.

The angle of his face put his neck on full display. He balled his fist in the sheet covering his bunk when her fingertip traced one of the bright lines from the underside of his jaw to where it disappeared beneath the collar of his shirt. "I wish we had time for me to hear all the stories behind these. I wonder what they mean to you."

Austin was about to promise they could have as long as she would give him.

Until she surprised him by admitting, "I have a tattoo. Just one, though I'd like more someday."

"Oh yeah, you told me that before." He snapped his head back in her direction, wondering where she wore her artwork. "What of? Can I see it?"

Hayden peeked from beneath thick lashes, then she nodded shyly. "It's a reminder to myself to stay positive even when things suck. Otherwise I can get sucked under and drown in negativity. Then it could never get better, which is way worse."

She walked the hem of her T-shirt up her concave belly. The creamy skin she exposed had him shifting restlessly. When she gathered the fabric just below her fantastic tits and arched away from him so he could see her side, he stiffened.

Partially because her tattoo was gorgeous. Colorful and bold, it molded to her body and made him itch to lick along every curve and line. Also because it was unintentionally shaded by a wicked bruise across her protruding ribs.

She needed to eat more. And get beat up less.

Fuck!

Austin clenched his jaw to keep from roaring. He swallowed his outrage and swore he'd make sure her ex paid for every bit of damage he'd done to Hayden. Mentally and physically. It took every ounce of his control to guarantee not a single fleck of pity showed in his gaze. Hayden braced herself, as if waiting for it.

How could he do that to her when the ink itself explained that she wouldn't appreciate it?

He read the elaborate cursive that swirled around a Victorian-styled clipper ship. "All the water in the ocean can't sink a ship unless you let it inside.'"

Well, damn. He supposed that was true, though easier said than done.

"I see your flag is still raised on the mast." He brushed his thumb over the waving banner, careful not to hurt her. "I guess that means you don't intend to surrender?"

"I can't believe you got that." She lifted her hand to his cheek and angled his chin so that he was staring into her face instead of at her tattoo. "I can't believe you get *me*."

When she put it like that, the arguments he'd had with himself over what was proper or wise flew out the truck's window. Because his gut was telling him that this was the moment.

"Let me know if I'm getting this part wrong..." He dipped his head slowly, giving her plenty of time to evade his advances. Instead, she met him more than halfway.

Hayden stretched up and snaked her hand around the nape of his neck, drawing him closer.

The first moment their lips touched, he felt an overwhelming rightness ground him. This wasn't a precursor to something more. Usually, for him, making out was the first step in a list of acts that graduated to full-on fucking. Sharing a kiss with Hayden was so much more than a stepping stone. Satisfying in its own right. Intimate as sin.

He cared more about comforting her, celebrating her, than he did about the physical pleasure of the act. Fuck, that wasn't a bad consolation prize, though.

Apparently, Hayden thought so too. She moaned softly as she ramped up their exchange from a mere brush of their lips to something far more intense. Kissing her was a full-contact sport.

She rose to her knees, then flung one over his thighs so that she straddled him. His hands naturally lifted to steady her. If they landed so his palms cupped her ass, holding her in place as they fused their mouths, it was only for her safety. Tumbling out of his bunk wouldn't be good for her injuries. Right?

That twisted logic had him slamming on the brakes. Whoa. What was he thinking?

Austin raised his hands to her shoulders and eased her back until their lips and tongues separated with a slick sound that did absolutely nothing to keep his stiff dick in check.

Flushed cheeks and bright eyes looked good on Hayden. So did the lust-dazed stare she gave him as they caught their breath. He'd guessed they shared some intense chemistry, but even he had been unprepared for the explosion they produced when they collided.

Before he did something unwise, he settled Hayden on the far side of his bunk, then rose from the bed and collected his camping gear from the cabinet where he'd stowed it that morning. He took his cowboy hat off the peg on the side of the cabinet and plopped it onto his head.

Hayden reached toward him. "Hey, Austin?"

"Yeah."

"Why don't you stay a little longer? Sleep in here tonight. With me." She'd turned the tables on him, stealing his favorite line.

Austin's blatant hard-on begged him to misunderstand and assume she meant it as an invitation to fuck. The wiser part of his mind knew otherwise. She was being polite and unknowingly testing his self-control.

"There's not exactly a lot of room in here. But the passenger seat probably is more comfortable than the trailer. Hell, the floor would be a step up. At least it's got carpet." He paused. "You're sure?"

She shook her head. "No."

Austin understood. He headed toward the door instead.

Hayden rocked onto her knees and one hand. With the other, she reached out and grabbed a fistful of his shirt. "I mean you're not sleeping on the damn floor of your own rig. We're adults. Give me your sleeping bag and I'll stay on top of the covers. We can even face opposite directions if it's too weird for you after I pretty much just attacked you."

"*Weird*? I'm trying to be fucking chivalrous here." He took his hat off and raked his hand through his hair.

At first, he thought the huffs of air escaping from her were sobs, and he felt awful for cursing at her or making her feel like her passion was unreciprocated. Until he realized she was laughing through the hand clapped over her open mouth.

Silently at first, and then in loud barks that culminated with an adorable snort before she wiped moisture from the corner of her eyes. "Well, I think you got halfway there. Other than your filthy mouth, your mom would be proud of you."

That last bit sounded mostly serious.

Of course she didn't know his mind had fixated on *filthy* and was thinking of the many, many ways he could prove her right about that.

The night would be a blend of heaven and hell. Sure, why not?

Austin dropped his gear in the passenger seat then vaulted onto the bunk. "Fine then, I'm staying. But there's no need for you to use my sleeping bag. I'm pretty sure you don't have cooties, and I'm man enough to keep my dick in my pants while holding you. If that's what you want."

She practically melted in front of his eyes, diving beneath his covers and burrowing into his pillow. He wondered how long the sheets would smell like her and the strawberry scent of the shampoo he'd picked out. "Is it pathetic to admit I think I *need* it? After everything that's happened, another night by myself sounds like torture when I could spend it with you instead."

"If it is then we're both losers, because the thought of deserting you in here or dropping you off at a hotel was tearing me up." Austin flipped off the lights then climbed in beside her. Like a pet cat, she curled up beside him, fitting herself into the curves and angles of his body. "This is much better."

"Mmm," she practically purred. "Much."

Neither of them spoke for a while after that. He tried to process how events had led to this and what it would take to keep them pointed in the right direction. He could get used to a traveling partner like Hayden. Especially if he didn't have to worry about every moment being the last one he might get to enjoy with her.

"Hayden?" he murmured before he could think better of it.

"Hmm?" She had nearly fallen asleep already. Exhaustion, the chaos of the day, a full belly, and their combined body heat were probably reasons enough for that. Some small part of him prayed it might also be because she instinctively trusted him to keep her safe.

Given where she'd come from, he knew that was a weighty responsibility for him and extremely brave of her. So he repaid her faith in kind. He put himself out there. "You don't have to answer me tonight. Just sleep on this…"

His deep inhalation whistled through his teeth as she blinked up at him in the glow from the streetlamps that filtered through his curtains.

Then he said, "Come with me to Compass Ranch in the morning. Stay, just a little bit longer, until you find your dad. You're going to have to live someplace until then. Why not with me? You'll be safe there. Your ex will never find you. And it won't cost you anything, like a hotel or a short-term apartment would. If you're not comfortable with that arrangement I guarantee you Hope or one of my cousins would love for you to be their guest instead. There's probably even work for you there to help build up your kitty some more."

"That's tempting. God, it is." She hid her face against his chest when she mumbled, "But then your perfect, zany, storybook family will wonder why you dragged home someone as messed up as me."

"I promise, they'll love you as much as I…" He cleared his throat. "You know what I mean. In a generic sense, not in a creepy way. There's nothing wrong with you, Hayden, and everything wrong with the fucker who made you doubt that. I know my family. Every single one of them would be with me on that."

She patted his chest, dismissing the graceless way he'd

stuffed his boot in his mouth at such a critical moment. Worse, she didn't agree outright. "We'll see."

Then again, she didn't say no either. He'd take it.

"Fair enough." He stole one tiny kiss. A simple press of his lips to hers. No tongue. No groping. And it was still enough to set him on fire. "Sleep tight, okay?"

"I have a feeling that's not going to be a problem." She yawned again, her voice already fading as the bedding absorbed their combined heat and reflected it back.

At least one of them should get some rest. Austin would be awake the entire night, memorizing the feel of her pressed against him in case it was the last time he got to experience it. Though they weren't as close as he would have liked, she fit perfectly in his arms.

She trusted him to protect her.

For now, that was enough.

Tomorrow was different story.

13

Hayden gripped the door handle, her palms sweaty. How had she gotten talked into coming all the way to Wyoming with Austin?

Just a little bit longer and a little bit longer…that's how.

Gradually he'd coaxed her into staying, with tiny commitments that made sense when considered individually. About to be transported onto his family's ranch, she would be the only thing mucking up its perfection.

It was hard to ignore the grin on his face or how he sped up as they rounded curves he'd learned to drive on. The hand-painted sign they'd passed about five minutes ago had proclaimed Compass Ranch was just a few miles down the road. There were no other stops between here and the place and people he loved so much.

Austin snapped her out of her mounting terror when he admitted, "My parents are going to freak out. I've never brought a woman home with me before."

"Wait." She froze. "You're not going to introduce me to them, are you?"

"Why the hell wouldn't I?" He took his eyes from the road to squint at her as if she'd lost her mind.

"Because they might get the wrong idea. I'm not staying. And, well..." She waved her fingers at her face, which had blossomed into even more violent shades of purple with hints of a sickly yellow that morning. "I look like this."

"Like a survivor?"

"Like someone who makes bad decisions." She cleared her throat and peered out the side window instead of at him. Fertile, thriving land rolled by. No wonder his family had settled here and made so much out of it.

"Hey, it's okay. I'm not going to pressure you to do anything you're not comfortable with. I promise they would adore you, but I get it if that's just too much right now. I have my own place on the ranch. You're welcome to stay there as long as you like." He reached over and squeezed her hand.

She nodded.

They were quiet then until he pulled through an unmarked turn that seemed to be a back entrance to the ranch. She appreciated that, since rolling up to the front door in his rig would have drawn attention she couldn't evade.

He stopped on a hard-packed dirt patch beside a brick red barn with white trim that looked like it had been there since the days his grandfather JD ran the place. Smaller than the horse stable he'd told her about, it seemed like it wasn't used much except maybe for storage. Was this where he parked his truck when he wasn't working?

"Would you mind opening the bay for me?" He tossed her a key, which she snatched out of the air. Glad to be of use for once, she climbed down from the truck and stretched, trying not to wince at the stiffness in her ribs. It was better than the steady ache that had been there before, but still sore.

She trotted over to the door, unlocked it, then gritted her teeth as she yanked it open. Though it was huge, it rolled easily on well-greased hinges. When the way was clear, Austin inched forward, somehow managing to park perfectly in the tight spot.

After shutting the bay and securing it, he joined her. The solid hold he took on her elbow felt familiar already. Welcome. He used it to guide her around the corner.

"Come on up." He opened a door in the side wall, revealing a steep set of stairs that culminated in a landing and an antique door.

"You live in a barn?" She tilted her head as she studied the gorgeous weathered planks of the exterior. It had stood up to many storms in its existence. "That's not a criticism, by the way. I lived in a shack. This is way nicer. It has a certain...flair."

"Thanks and, technically, yes." Austin held his hand out to her and she took it. They climbed up to what would probably have been a hayloft back in the day. "My cousins and I completely renovated it the summer after I bailed out of college. I was thrilled to come back, but I needed my own apartment. No twenty-year-old really wants to live with their parents, do they?"

"I suppose not." She had chosen independence, too. That had obviously been a mistake. When he unlocked the door at the top of the stairs and ushered her into his space, she whispered, "Holy cow."

"None of those live here these days. Just me, sorry." He looked around as if seeing his home with fresh eyes while she took it in for the first time.

Wide reclaimed lumber, whitewashed and distressed, warmed the entire place. Rustic furniture, an antique book collection, plush area rugs, and a variety of plants added to the inviting atmosphere. It seemed like a secret nook where she could hide. Forever, if necessary.

Suddenly, she was afraid that's exactly what Austin's apartment could become for her if they let it—a sanctuary where she could withdraw from the world and huddle in the corner without really making any of the progress she'd hoped for when she'd bolted from Bobby Joe and the unsatisfying life she'd been trapped in.

Hayden trailed Austin through his kitchen, admiring the open-concept living area. "These retro appliances are amazing. They really fit in here."

"Funny enough, they were stashed in the barn. We found them when we were cleaning it out and realized they still worked. It seemed smart to save money at the time. Now I can't imagine it with modern ones." He pointed to a photograph on the wall. In it a handsome cowboy twirled a young woman wearing an apron around in her kitchen. The fabric of her skirt billowed, showing a hint of her fabulous legs beneath. "That's Vivi and JD. You can see this oven in the background."

Hayden couldn't explain why such a happy moment frozen in time caused tears to sting her eyes. Maybe because she had believed she'd found something that would last a lifetime and longer, but it hadn't even endured a decade. She dragged the tip of her finger across the white enamel edge of the stove before joining Austin in his cozy living room.

"I get that you'd rather have peace right now and don't want to go see my parents." He massaged the back of her neck gently, letting her know he really did understand. "But would you mind if I ran over to the main house to tell my parents and Jake that I'm home and let them know the trip went fine?"

For her it had gone better than fine. She'd fled into the night with nothing, yet somehow ended up here, with him and the chance at a new life. She wouldn't deny him anything, especially not such a simple request. "Of course not. I didn't mean to keep you from them."

"You're not." He reached down and bracketed her shoulders in his palms. The series of simple touches drove her mad as she recalled what it had felt like as he'd kissed her the night before. "I won't abandon you in a strange place. I'll just be a little while, okay? My computer is on the desk over there. Feel free to start doing some research and trying to catch up with your dad. Or go lie down and rest if you'd rather. Make yourself at home. There's a messaging app on the laptop. You can reach me through it if you need anything. I'll see it on my phone. Okay?"

"Sure, that sounds perfect." She smiled softly as his heat soaked into her bones. The memory of sharing that warmth with him the night before heated her further.

Hayden rose onto her tiptoes and stole another taste to hold her over until his return. Plus it felt like he deserved a reward for being so damn gracious. He kept his hands stuffed in his pockets as he kissed her, but the sensual rake of his teeth over her bottom lip as her heels sank back to the aged floorboards made it clear that there was a lot more to him than she'd seen so far.

Was she ready for Austin to unleash himself? Probably not.

At least one of them had some self control.

"See you soon," he rasped, and tipped his hat in her direction before slipping from the apartment. She listened to his boot-steps as they descended the stairs, then spied on him through the giant octagonal window in the dining nook as he strode across the grass in the direction of his parents' house. She could easily stare at him all day.

When he disappeared from view, she sighed and turned to his computer.

If she didn't start looking for her dad soon, she might forget why she should. Was she making the same mistake again? Trusting a man too much? Putting too much faith in him? Counting on him to take care of her when she was plenty capable of fending for herself?

Damn it! She'd better get to work.

14

———

Austin couldn't say why it was that he felt anxious approaching his parents' house. It was like the time he'd admitted to them he'd dropped out of school. Except he hadn't done anything wrong. Well, honestly, he hadn't then either, but he had been about to tell them about something that would change the course of his life.

Could his run-in with Hayden be in the same category of events?

It seemed silly to make that proclamation so soon, despite the undeniable attraction between them. Something in his gut was leaning that way, though. He needed to talk to his parents —Jake too—about her. Deep down, he dreaded them popping his rosy bubble.

Jake's truck was in the yard. Maybe he would take Austin's side again like he had five years ago, or maybe he'd say that Austin was nuts to be so infatuated with a woman he'd only known a few days, who came with a crap ton of baggage despite having nothing to her name.

He wiped his sweaty palms on his jeans. The screen door

squeaked a bit when he yanked it open harder than intended. *Oops. Settle down.*

"I'm back," he called as he headed for the kitchen.

"Hey!" Jake waved from his spot at the table with a half-eaten biscuit in his hand. "How'd the run go?"

"Good." Even to him, his response sounded unsure.

Lucy peeked from around the open fridge door, her mom senses putting her on instant alert. "What's going on? Did you have an accident? Are you okay?"

She rushed to him and looked him over from head to toe. He hugged her and laughed. "Mom, I'm fine. Really. Nobody died, damn."

"So the calves made the trip fine then?" His father tended to think of the ranch business first and let Lucy and Colby handle more of the emotional stuff. It didn't offend Austin—he knew his father showed affection in his own ways.

"Yep. The buyer already told me he could use double next time if we've got them. He was really impressed with the stock." Austin put his hands in his back pockets and wandered over to the table.

"Of course he was," his dad said as he smiled at Austin's father. "Silas only sells the best. Now come here and give me a hug."

Hey, Austin might be a twenty-four-year-old man, but when Colby embraced him and slapped him on the back, it helped ease some of his tension.

His mother still eyed him as she wrung her hands. She wasn't easily fooled.

Jake hid a smirk behind his fist. "Can I guess?"

Austin kicked out a chair beside the guy and sank into it. "Sure, why not? It's only my personal life we're kidding about."

"Your face has woman trouble written all over it." Jake shoved the rest of the biscuit in his mouth and chomped it down in two chews. The guy ate like a farm hand, that was for sure.

"How do you always know everything?" Silas asked Jake with a shake of his head. "You should have been a private eye instead of a rancher. Or maybe the town gossip."

"I'm wise beyond my years."

"Jake, you're seventy. How much wiser can you get, buddy?" Colby barked out a laugh.

Jake shrugged. "To be fair, I heard it from Cathy and Emily Haley. They were rearranging the window display of their new boutique in town when Austin stopped at the light. Cathy asked me who the pretty girl with the sad eyes was. I sure didn't know. But I think I'm about to find out."

"Well, yeah. I brought a girl home with me." Austin grimaced. In Compton Pass, like a lot of small towns, he could take a shit, barely finish wiping his ass, and the neighbor three farms over would know before he'd flushed the toilet.

"You have a girlfriend?" Colby probed.

Austin didn't know how to explain. "I wouldn't really call her that."

Though he might like to steer them in that direction. She'd shown her true colors in one of the worst times of her life. Everything she'd laid out, he admired and respected. Hayden appealed to him in so many ways—her personality, her determination, her looks, and definitely the chemistry they shared.

He tried not to think of their kiss while his parents were staring at him.

"Kid, spit it out," his father demanded. "This isn't like you. Why are you being evasive?"

"Because I'm not sure where to draw the line on respecting her privacy and getting your advice on the situation. See, she didn't exactly want to come here. But she didn't have a lot of options either. Well, no options really."

Jake narrowed his eyes. "Are you keeping her chained to your bed or something? I mean, that seemed to work out for your uncle Seth. So what do I know? I guess I should have tried that with Haiwee."

Austin laughed, simultaneously horrified to think of his aunt Jody in that legendary kinky situation and bummed since it probably wasn't a smart tactic to use on Hayden given her history. He'd have to try something slightly more subtle.

"Are you telling us you picked up a hitchhiker?" Lucy put her fingers over her mouth. "Austin, what would make you take a chance like that?"

"Uh...actually...she's a stowaway." He hoped that didn't make them think badly of her.

"That poor girl." Colby, always the most sensitive, immediately thought of Hayden. "Whatever scared her into doing that had to be pretty fucked up."

"An abusive boyfriend," Austin groaned as he remembered the dark splotches marring her skin. "He beat her up pretty good, that fucker. She's lucky she got free of him. It was night. All she had on was a baggy T-shirt. She hid in the trailer and... well... Now she's here."

"Jesus. Is she all right?" Jake gawked. "I bet it was cold as the meat locker back there. Please tell me it was only for a few minutes and then she got your attention somehow."

Austin shook his head. "An entire damn day. She's okay, though. Mostly. She's tough. And resilient. And...*really* fucking pretty. Her name is Hayden and I think she could use a bunch of your cooking, Mom."

He put his face in his hands, thinking again of everything that could have happened to her. What if she'd fallen out and he'd run over her? He felt sick even imagining it.

"Why didn't she come with you then? Was she afraid we'd judge her?" Lucy stood as if she planned to march directly to his house, feed Hayden, then hug the shit out of her until she realized the Comptons weren't like that.

It might not have been the worst plan ever, to be honest. It's sort of what he'd been aiming for.

"Maybe some," he admitted. "I think she's like you and Hope and the rest of the girls. Proud, fierce, and independent. Pretty sure she's blaming herself over this or some shit. How can I show her that it's okay to lean on me and that it doesn't make her weak?"

"Oh boy." Jake put his hand on Austin's shoulder and squeezed. "You have a thing for her already?"

No use in denying it. "Yeah. A big thing."

Jake punched Austin's biceps. "Don't get nasty. That's certainly not going to work on the young lady."

"Hey!" Austin put his hands up. "I didn't even mean it like that. You're the one with the dirty mind."

"That's pretty much the only benefit of being old. I get to be a dirty old man. Don't try to take my rights away, whippersnapper," Jake shook his finger at Austin.

Silas grinned at Austin while Lucy and Colby pretended they weren't hearing the conversation, especially at the dinner table.

"So...anyway, I told her she could stay with me until she finds her dad. He got remarried. They had a falling out and lost touch, but he's all she has."

"That's rough." Jake's eyes misted over as if he was remembering his past. "Those wounds are a lot harder to heal than some bumps and bruises. Sometimes you can never bridge those gaps once they're created. You're going to have to be ready to support her if she finds out this is one of those times. Whatever you do, don't put yourself between her and her family, even if they turn out to be toxic. Take it from me. That's a no-win proposition."

Austin finally felt like he had an inkling of how deep a loss like that would cut. Jake was even stronger than he'd thought. He was damn near a cowboy superhero.

"When she's ready, we'd love to meet Hayden." His mom squeezed him tight. It sometimes felt strange that she barely came up to his chest these days. "She sounds like she'd fit right in here."

"I'm hoping she will," Austin sighed. "If she hasn't already run away."

"You'd better get back to her," Colby said. "She's got to be scared. You're her lifeline. The only person she knows and trusts right now. Even if she wasn't ready for all of our nonsense, she probably doesn't need to be alone for too long."

Silas tossed in his two cents. "Listen to your dad. He's good at this stuff. But if the gentle touch doesn't work, be prepared to fight for her. Don't be an idiot, like me, and give up on what you want because it seems impossible."

"It's the thing most worth fighting for in this life," Jake agreed. "Even if you're not completely sure yet where this thing is going, it's worth doing your damnedest to find out rather than learning later that you could have been so much more to her than you were. Trust me on that, kid."

"Thanks." Austin slapped Jake on the back, shocked when the impact of his hand rocked the guy forward some. He'd have to be more careful from now on.

His mom packed Hayden and him about twelve-people's worth of food before his parents sent him on his way, more determined to follow his heart, no matter how crazy the damn thing might be.

15

Hayden sank into the wooden desk chair she'd bet also came out of the storage area in the barn below. It had character that most newer, factory-made furniture didn't. Attention to detail and charming inconsistencies showed someone had crafted it with their own skills instead of a computer or a laser.

Right off the bat, she tried emailing her father at the last known email address she had for him. Like it had last time she'd attempted to reach out, her message failed and came back instantly. Automatically.

So she spent the better part of an hour scouring the internet for any hint of his whereabouts. None of the searches on his name turned up people who looked like him, even taking into account the effect of the years that had passed since he'd left her behind.

Eventually she blew out a sigh and studied the impressive raw beams of the apartment's sloped ceiling. There was only one other thing she could think of to try. Brenda, her father's new wife, who probably wasn't actually the Cuntess of Cuntington like Hayden's immature mind had made her out to be. She had the woman's email address from the lame attempt they'd made to get to know each other before everything had imploded and the silent treatment on both sides had engaged.

Still, she kept her note brief and to the point. *I need to speak with my father. Please ask him to call me at his earliest convenience. Thank you—Hayden.*

She hoped Austin wouldn't mind that she copied and pasted his cell number from the messaging-slash-videochat app he'd told her he used. It was the only reliable communication she had at the moment.

Her finger trembled as it hovered over the button that would send her SOS. If there was any other option, she'd take it. Angry at herself, her father, Bobby Joe, and the world in general, she brought her finger down. Sent.

As she sat there for a moment, head in hands, she debated crashing on the couch. Although it was early, she was exhausted. She'd spent a lot of the night awake, though resting, in Austin's arms. It had seemed impossible to drift off when she was burning up inside. His hard-on had imprinted itself on her hip, but he hadn't made any move to put it to better use. So she had pretended like she hadn't noticed it or her own matching desire. It was probably some reflexive instinct anyway. Maybe she'd have been attracted to anyone who'd rescued her.

A nap sounded amazing.

Right before she closed the lid of Austin's laptop, a bleep notified her of an incoming message. A handsome guy's face appeared in a flashing circle in the center of the screen. The text below it proclaimed it was Austin's cousin Bryant.

She tried to swipe it out of the way but must have poked it instead.

The screen flashed *connecting*.

Oh fuck! Her options now were to hang up or explain. In the split second she had to decide, she tried to consider her options. Austin had offered to introduce her to his family. So he wouldn't mind if she answered, would he?

Nah, she didn't think so.

He'd probably prefer that to her being rude to his cousins.

Besides, she was dying of curiosity and it seemed like a safe way to ease the unexpected loneliness creeping up on her without Austin around. In the silence of Austin's deserted apartment, it was too easy to remember that until she reconnected with her dad, it was her versus the world.

Her panic intensified when the screen split into four squares. Each one held a face—three smoking hot guys who bore a slight resemblance to Austin, and herself.

"Hey shithead! Why haven't you called—"

"Good job, Doug," James said before he and Bryant roared with laughter as they realized the mistake their cousin had made by talking before the program had fully connected. "Go ahead and insult Austin's new lady friend. I'm sure it won't hurt that much when he kicks your ass for it."

Hayden laughed. "I won't tell if you don't tell him I accidentally answered you guys instead of closing the app. He went to let his parents and Jake know that he's home."

"He wouldn't give a shit that you're talking to us." Doug eased her anxiety.

"You didn't go with Austin because..." James wondered.

She shrugged. "It's complicated."

"Would you really want to be surrounded by all those nosey strangers at once?" Bryant asked his cousin as he waved his hands in front of his chest. "No, thank you."

"Well, you got the better end of the deal anyway," Doug said. "We're a lot more fun to talk to."

"Sexier to look at, too," James added.

"Ignore those idiots." Bryant came to her rescue, though it wasn't really necessary. Hayden's face ached from grinning so wide already. They were fun and easygoing like Austin. She bet they had no trouble at all finding women to entertain. "How are you? Do you need anything since you're there alone?"

"Oh! I know!" Doug jumped in. "Check the second drawer on your left."

"I don't think I should rummage around in Austin's desk." Even she had some boundaries. She'd invaded pretty much all of his personal space already.

"It's fine," Bryant assured her. Somehow she knew he wouldn't lead her astray. He seemed a little more reserved than his cousins. She could tell from the way he spoke as much as the stories Austin had shared. "Go ahead."

So she did.

"A chocolate stash!" She grinned. "Hell yes! You guys are the best."

They cracked up as she plucked a mini candy bar from the jar and unwrapped it. Hayden swept her hair out of her eyes and tucked it behind her ear so that she could pop the candy into her mouth. She instantly regretted it.

James growled as Doug unleashed a steady stream of profanity including some curses she'd never heard before. Bryant winced and said, "Oh, honey. That had to hurt. I'm so, so sorry."

She angled the chair so that her undamaged side was visible to the camera, then went back for a second helping of sweets. Her audience didn't seem to hold it against her.

When she looked up again, her shame was burned off by the trio of fierce, protective, honorable men who pegged her with a concerned stare very similar to the ones Austin had been giving her for days now. They truly were alike in all the ways that counted.

"There's probably ice cream in the freezer, if that helps," Bryant offered.

They were saved an awkward conversation then because Austin returned. He smiled when he crossed to her and saw she was chatting with his cousins. "I see you've met the rest of the Compass Boys."

"They're great, like you." She turned and put her arms around his waist. He ran his fingers through her hair, inspiring her to close her eyes and bury her cheek against his washboard abs for a moment. Maybe some of his strength would rub off on her.

"I can't believe you kept her," Doug blurted with a goofy grin, lightening the mood.

"Shit. She's not a puppy!" Austin crouched beside her so that he was at eye level with the laptop's camera. He put one hand on her knee—maybe for balance, maybe because he could sense something wasn't quite right. "She needed somewhere to lay low for a while."

"And it doesn't hurt that she's sexy as fuck." James peered into the screen as if trying to see what might be blossoming between them.

Hayden would like to figure that out for herself. Confused and overwhelmed, she decided a nap was definitely in her near future. If she was lucky, Austin would join her.

He joked around with his cousins for a while, letting her unwind as she listened to their banter. It startled her when he jerked.

"Something bite you?" Doug asked with a laugh.

"Nah, it's my phone, vibrating. Someone's calling." He took it from his pocket and glared at the screen. "Nobody I know. Unidentified caller. Probably a telemarketer or some crap."

He swiped it off his screen and sent it to voicemail as the guys began to debate who was going to win that night's baseball game. Hayden loved eavesdropping on their exchange and witnessing how they ragged on each other without any real malice. She pictured what it might be like if she had a close-knit group of friends like that to share the highs and lows of her life with.

"Damn." Austin picked up his phone as it began ringing again. "Persistent fucker. Hang on. Let me get rid of them quick."

"Can I help you?" His stern tone shocked her. He sounded nothing like the man she'd gotten to know. Hayden wouldn't want to mess with someone like that. It would probably be best to remember that although he'd never been anything but gentle and kind with her, he had the capacity for something meaner.

"Oh. Uh, yeah. Sorry. She's right here." His gaze whipped to her as his brows drew together. "Hold on one second."

Austin held the phone out to her. Her stomach bottomed out. Only one person knew to reach her at his number.

"My dad?" She reached for it, her arms shaking as her hands turned icy.

He shook his head and said quietly, "No, it's a woman."

Brenda. Was her father so angry that he refused even to speak to her? Or had that bitch decided not to pass along her request? Hayden wasn't sure she was ready to have this conversation.

"Go ahead." Austin shook the phone at her. "You've got this. I'm right here."

He wrapped her fingers around the cell, then waved to his cousins before severing their connections. Not before she saw three very concerned faces staring back at them, though. Damn it!

She swallowed hard, gathered her courage, and croaked, "Brenda?"

"Hayden! I am so surprised. I never expected to hear from you." Why did it sound like that sort of made Brenda sad? She'd never been overtly rude, despite Hayden's juvenile reactions to her dad falling in love and uprooting their micro-family, but Brenda had never seemed eager to inherit another man's daughter either. Maybe her dad had suffered, as she had, in her absence.

Had they both been too stubborn to overcome their rift?

Hayden suddenly felt foolish for wasting so much time.

"I'm sorry. I wouldn't have bothered you, except it's an emergency. Can I talk to my dad?" Hayden chewed the nail of her middle finger. When Austin drew her onto his lap, she was glad for the security and weight of his arms around her.

"Is this a joke?" Brenda sounded less welcoming now.

"No, I really need to speak with him. Please." Her voice cracked. She hated having to ask for something that should have been her right as his child.

"Hayden, you're scaring me." Brenda sounded every bit as upset as Hayden was. "How would I know where he is?"

"Because you're his wife? Because he left me for you? Because..."

"What?" the other woman whispered. There was a crash, as if she had fallen to her knees on the floor. "Hayden, your dad chose you. Why don't you know where he is? Why are you asking me about him? I haven't seen him in five years, since he pulled into my driveway long enough to tell me that you had to be his number one priority. He kissed me goodbye, turned right around, and went back to you. I never heard from him again."

Hayden couldn't move. Couldn't talk. Couldn't breathe.

"Are you still there?" Brenda asked, crying openly now. "What's going on?"

Austin gripped Hayden tightly enough that she couldn't slip to the ground. He began to rock her as what Brenda told her sank in. There was no chance her father had abandoned both of the people he had loved most.

Something horrible had happened.

And no one had known. No one had been there to help him.

Hayden might not have the facts about how or why, but she was certain.

Her dad was gone forever.

It took a minute to realize that the screaming she heard was coming from her own mouth. Pain bubbled up from her guts then exploded through her lungs. She couldn't stop it. When the first rush subsided, her shriek morphed into sobs.

Austin took the phone from her. "I'll have her contact you when she's able."

He disconnected then tossed the phone onto the couch before scooping Hayden into his arms. He stood, carrying her to his bedroom. "Jesus Christ, I'm so sorry. Oh God, I'm sorry."

She couldn't do anything except cling to him and bawl.

Every muscle in her body tensed to the breaking point.

A coughing fit interrupted her wails. Agony seared her side. At first she thought it was her cracked ribs protesting until she realized it went deeper than that. And when she raised her hand to wipe her mouth, it came away speckled with blood.

Hayden's eyes widened. She turned her palm to face Austin, who cursed. It became impossible to catch her breath between crying, coughing, grief, and terror. The room dimmed.

Using the last of her air, she whispered, "Help."

"Hayden!" Austin shook her, which only made the pain worse. "Holy shit."

He left her on the bed to sprint for the other room and, presumably, his phone. Because the last thing she heard was him shouting, "Hope! It's an emergency. Get over to my apartment now. I'm calling 911, but you'll get here first. Hurry. Please."

Hayden gasped and shuddered. She tried desperately to claw her way to consciousness, but she couldn't make it. Panic set in. Everything hurt. Her heart, her body. She was tired of fighting. Weary.

So she surrendered and let the darkness have her.

16

———————

A gentle female voice kept encouraging Hayden to emerge from her sleep and the bad dreams plaguing her. "That's right, open your eyes."

"Is she okay?" Austin asked. "Hope, what's going on?"

Hayden roused, trying to tell him not to worry. It didn't sound good on him.

"Her blood pressure is coming back to normal and her airway is clear. She needs to go in for a full evaluation, including an endoscopy. But from what you told me, and what I see, I think she's going to be fine. Exhaustion, a stomach full of ulcers, possible anemia, and shock are my guess. They're going to run some tests and probably keep her for observation."

"I'm fine," Hayden insisted, or tried to. It came out as more of a moan.

She attempted to sit up. Austin and Hope double-teamed her, pinning her shoulders to the lush mattress.

He wasn't having any of it. "Oh no, you're not. And you're staying right there until the paramedics come and get you. I'm about to give you a tour of Compton Pass's hospital."

"I don't have insurance." She shook her head. "Just let me sleep this off. It was just... Oh God, my dad."

Her breathing hitched once more.

"I know, I know." Austin climbed into bed and snaked himself around her. "But you have to stay calm, okay?"

"Inhale, slow and deep. Let it out slowly," Hope reminded Hayden. "You hyperventilated."

Hayden nodded, causing tears to spill down her cheeks.

"Maybe you should give her some space before you suffocate her, Austin." The deep, calm voice of a man jolted Hayden. She hadn't realized there was anyone else in the room.

"That's just my husband, Clay." Hope smiled at Hayden, doing a great job of distracting her and giving her body a chance to settle itself. "My other husband, Wyatt, is outside, waiting for the ambulance."

She craned her neck and lifted her blurry gaze for a glimpse of one of the people Austin had told her so much about.

"Hey," Clay said as he lifted a calloused hand in greeting, though his face was somber.

"You're taller than I pictured," she told him, her mouth completely unfiltered at the moment.

The man shot Austin a WTF look. They probably thought she was completely insane at this point. Hell, maybe she was.

Austin barked out a distressed laugh, then hugged her. He didn't bother filling them in about how he'd lured her there with stories about them. Somehow feeling safer in the presence of not only Austin but also the man who'd protected his wife against a mob in a bar brawl once-upon-a-time, Hayden was able to take a deep breath, and then another.

"That's better," Hope said as she patted Hayden's hand.

Hayden couldn't keep up with the flurry of emotions that continued to rain down on her after an already wickedly unsteady week. Shock and grief over her dad, physical pain, intense attraction, admiration and envy of the Compton clan, fear for her future, and now the realization that she was utterly alone in life.

It was too much.

Though she didn't lose it like she had before, she turned into Austin's side and let bucketfuls of tears drain from her. She drenched his plaid shirt as he tried to convince her things were going to be okay. She couldn't even get them to stop when sirens approached and new arrivals crowded Austin's cozy apartment.

Despite her weak arguments, she caved to Austin's demands when he insisted she let them take her away for tests and treatment.

At least he never once let go of her hand.

Not even when his uncle Sawyer, the town's sheriff, appeared at her hospital bedside to tell her that Brenda's local police had taken a statement that allowed them to pinpoint the date of his disappearance. It coincided with a fatal accident involving an unidentified man driving an unregistered van that matched the description of the one her dad had bought secondhand just before packing his life up for his new beginning. One he'd never made because of her.

After another meltdown, the nurses on staff pumped Hayden full of anti-anxiety medication that made her foggy and sleepy, comfortably numb.

Even then, Austin didn't leave her alone. Every time she blinked her eyes open through the night, he was beside her bed, his fingers interlocked with hers. The next day, he waited for the doctor to review her test results and formulate a treatment plan to start healing her wounds from the inside out before clearing her for discharge.

He might as well have written a prescription for time with Austin instead.

The man's unwavering support and presence kept her

grounded during some of the toughest moments of her life. He promised over and over that things would get better and reminded her that she was strong enough to get back up again. And again. And again, if necessary.

She added it to the list of things she owed him dearly for—and never anticipated that she'd be able to repay the favor so soon in the future.

17

———

A few days later, Hayden was feeling well enough to venture out of the protective bubble of Austin's apartment and start to properly introduce herself to his family. He'd left early that morning to help out with a fencing project that required all the ranch hands out in one of the pastures. He thought they might be done before lunch but hadn't reappeared yet, so she decided to explore on her own.

She wrapped the last of the brownies she'd made in parchment paper then borrowed a pen from Austin's desk. She grabbed two sticky notes and wrote *Thank you!* on one and *Went to see your sister. Don't worry, I saved the best ones for you.* on the other. Then she drew a smiley face and an arrow. She set the second note on the counter and left the smaller packet of treats at the tip of it for Austin. Hopefully he liked the corner pieces as much as she did.

With a pat, she secured her note onto Hope's parcel, checked her hair and lip gloss in her distorted reflection on the refrigerator door, and left her sanctuary.

She'd studied an aerial shot of the ranch on an online satellite map. Between that and the stories Austin had told her, she was almost certain she knew which direction to head for Compass Girl Row, where Hope lived with her husbands. Maybe she should have made a double batch of brownies.

Ah well, she figured the guys had learned to share long ago.

Hurrying, she kept her head down as she weaved between sheds and vehicles parked in the ranch lot. When she noticed the doors to the giant horse barn were flung open, she couldn't resist a peek at the place so central to many of Austin's tales. It seemed most everyone else was out and about, doing whatever it was their job to do on the ranch. At midday, no one was here.

So she tiptoed inside, planning to cut through the structure on her stroll to Hope's house.

Hayden placed her palm on the central pillar as she looked around in awe. There had been weddings here. Fights. Hookups. Ranch meetings. Dances. All sorts of important moments.

Could this be a pivotal point in her own life?

Finding Austin had already altered her future. But how much exactly?

Over the past week they'd become inseparable. He'd encouraged her to concentrate exclusively on getting better. Now that she was moving in the right direction, it wouldn't be long until she had to make some tough decisions and start the next phase of her life, whatever that might look like.

Would it be wrong to make the most of their limited time together? Though they'd slept together the past several nights, nothing improper had happened despite her less than subtle hints that she'd be up for it if it did.

Tonight, she would attempt to be more persuasive.

What was wrong with blowing off steam with a man she was extremely attracted to? One who wouldn't tangle her in strings, and one she wouldn't ever see again after this too-brief intermission was over? He'd proved over and over that he would never hurt her. Intimacy with him would be unlike anything she'd ever experienced. Not that that was saying a lot since Bobby Joe was the only guy she'd ever been with and, well... Right.

Hayden drew a deep breath, then patted the support beam holding everything up. Holding it together. Right now, Austin was that solid structure in her life. What would happen when she didn't have him to rely on anymore?

"Hey, is that you?" Speak of the cowboy.

Hayden spun toward the back door. An enormous smile stretched her cheeks. It seemed like her face did it automatically whenever he was around. "Hi. I hope it's okay for me to be in here."

"Of course." He sauntered to her then wrapped her in his arms. "Is it everything I made it out to be?"

"Hmm...I'm not sure. I heard it's a pretty good spot to fool around. Why don't you show me the hayloft?" Hayden couldn't believe she'd been bold enough to ask.

"Did you mean that like it sounded?" His eyes darkened.

She nodded. "Uh huh."

Austin lunged for her. He tossed her over his shoulder then strode toward a ladder. She never did get to find out exactly how he planned to climb it while carrying her, though.

A groan stopped him in his tracks.

As they froze and listened, a shuffling came from a stall nearby.

Though it would have been wise to run away from whatever was causing the disturbance, Austin set her down gently then crept closer instead. She followed, coaching herself not to scream if a rat ran past.

It wasn't a rodent causing the disturbance.

A pair of weathered boots peeked out from an open door beside a pitchfork that looked as if it had fallen haphazardly. One of the boots slid against the dirt floor as if the person was attempting to stand or at least gain some traction.

"What the fuck?" Austin hissed as he bolted into the shadowy area.

Hayden ran after him, alarmed by the pitch of his voice.

"Shit shit shit!" Hearing the alarm ringing through his shout injected ice into Hayden's veins. If Austin, who wasn't afraid of anything, was scared...something was really wrong.

A strangled grunt was the only response. So she rushed in beside Austin, only to discover an elderly man lying on the ground. He'd obviously fallen there since his cowboy hat had flown off his head and landed a few feet away. His left hand clutched his skull. He moaned again.

Not the sort of moan you make when you're having a nightmare or the kind she'd sometimes heard from herself when her ulcers had been in full force. This was a horrible sound she'd never quite get out of her brain now that it had attacked her ears.

"Oh my God. Is he okay?" It was a stupid question since he writhed in agony. His long silver hair and beard along with the deep grooves in his leathery face made her pretty sure she knew who he was, too. "Jake?"

His eyes opened, unevenly. His mouth drooped on one side as he tried to talk.

Austin skidded to his knees beside the man. Leaning over him, she could barely make out his garbled question when he asked, "Who that? Angel?"

"I'm nobody." She crouched on his other side, grasping his hand. It was freezing. "Hang on. I'll get help."

"Don't go." His steely grip surprised her given the ashen cast to his face and his labored breathing. "Not dyin' alone."

"No, you're not doing that at all." Austin shook him slightly. "You're going to be fine. I'll call for Hope or someone. Viho. Anyone."

Hayden looked over her shoulder. There wasn't a single

person in the shady interior of the barn or outside its doors, in the bright sunlight.

"Give me your phone." She stuck out her hand in Austin's general direction and curled her fingers toward her palm a few times.

He tossed the device to her and she concentrated on stilling the violent trembling of her fingers long enough to dial 911. Was this how Austin had felt the other day?

Jake smiled softly at Austin before a grimace mangled half of the gentle curve of his lips. "Tell them all...I love them."

The man jackknifed up from the ground, his spine crimping as he dropped their fingers to clutch his head in both hands. He gasped. Flopped around some, scattering hay around him. Then went limp with his mouth cracked open. Eerily still.

It was his eyes that would haunt her. She saw them dilate as the life went out of him.

"Help!" Austin screamed despite the fact that no one would be able to change what had just happened. "Someone please help us!"

"Austin? Is that you?" A booming voice Hayden didn't recognize was followed by the thuds caused by someone running toward them.

Meanwhile the phone connected. She did her best to calmly relay pertinent information to the operator despite the chaos and confusion swirling around her.

"Viho! In here!" Austin hugged Jake tight, pressing his ear to the still man's chest. "I can't hear his heartbeat! Damn it. Jake! Come on!"

Hayden's own chest ached as she watched her rescuer fall apart.

It only got worse when a man with long, straight black hair and the most gorgeous, rich complexion she'd ever seen joined them. It was his eyes, though, that made her sure. This was Jake's biological son.

She made room for the man, who took cues from Austin. He put his hand in front of Jake's mouth, then groaned. "He's not breathing."

The men blinked utterly in shock. Seeing two such capable guys powerless, at a loss for what to do, killed her. She filled in the emergency responder, spelling out what she had seen as Viho ripped his father's shirt open and started administering CPR.

Austin helped as best he could. His motions were wooden and jerky.

Hayden didn't stop them. Didn't want there to be any doubt in their minds later.

The outcome wasn't about to change, though. They were cowboys, not miracle workers.

"He had a massive stroke. He..."

"No, don't say it!" Austin nudged Jake lightly. His surrogate grandfather's arms wiggled like the dead weight they were. "He can't be gone!"

Hayden turned her attention from Jake to Austin, who needed her a hell of a lot more right then. She stood behind him with her hand on his shoulder as he began to gasp. His back heaved. She thought he might get sick.

"The ambulance is on its way. I'm sending the coroner also," the operator informed her. "Do you need me to stay on the line until they get there?"

"Thank you, no." She hung up then, her sole focus on helping Austin survive the next few seconds, then minutes.

When Viho abandoned his efforts, Austin dove over Jake's body as if he was going to take up where his friend had left off. Viho stopped him with a firm grip on his forearm.

"He's gone, Austin. Stop." Viho's monotone command held no anger. "I...I swear I felt him leaving. That's why I came over here. I just had...a feeling. One I never want to have again. Like he was calling me."

"He said he loves you. All of you." Hayden's gaze wavered between Viho and Austin. She wished her arms were long enough to hold them both at the same time from opposite sides of the stall.

"Shit, no. No!" Austin bent in half, his forehead resting on Jake's shoulder, his fists pounding the ground until she feared they'd leave bloody streaks in the dirt.

Viho, on the other hand, bowed his head and began to chant in a native language that Hayden couldn't understand. Whatever he kept repeating sounded like a beautiful though heartrending sendoff for Jake's spirit.

One by one, other ranch hands trickled into the barn as they got wind of something happening.

Soon they crammed shoulder to shoulder behind Viho and Austin. Every last one of them took his hat off and stared as they said a silent farewell. Respect and sorrow oozed from each of the tough workers. Hayden's heart cracked more and more for Austin and his family.

The loss would be as devastating to their community as chopping down the center post of the barn would be to this building.

Austin looked up to meet her stare directly. He rose slowly to his feet. It freaked her out even more to see him blank out than it had when he'd erupted with motion. "Can you please go find my dads? There's a four-wheeler in the shed out back. The keys are in the seat. They're finishing up in the field near the ridge to the north. Drive along the fence line straight toward it. You won't miss them."

Though she hated to leave him, she'd do anything to get him through this. If he needed his family, she would bring them. "Of course. I'll be right back."

Hayden flung her arms around him and tried to hold him

as tightly as possible. He hugged her, too. Briefly, before he made a circuit around the tiny room. He kicked a bucket which made her jump when it clattered down the hall between the stalls. Then he returned to Jake's side as if he might suddenly think of something else to try. He didn't.

There wasn't anything a mere mortal could do. Jake's time had run out.

Hopefully Vicky and JD were there to welcome him, wherever he'd gone.

Austin spread his arms wide, grabbed the bars on the stall door, and let his head hang toward his chest. He croaked, "I can't believe this is real. Did this really just happen? What do I do now?"

He uttered words she'd thought herself often over the past week. First after her fight, the wild ride in Austin's truck, her performance at the Crispy Biscuit, learning her father had passed away, and now this. The blows kept coming.

"Austin." She raced to him and rubbed his back. It seemed to calm him some. "It did. I'm so sorry. I'm going to get your parents. They'll know what to do. Okay?"

She couldn't even give him the comfort of saying Jake hadn't suffered. Instead, she touched his face lightly and promised. "I'll go as fast as I can. And when I get back, I'm not leaving your side. Just like you never left mine. I'm here for you. Completely."

He would survive like she had, with the love and support of his family and friends, Hayden included. She turned to go.

Austin clasped her hand and lifted it to his mouth, pressing a kiss to her knuckles.

It broke her heart when his glassy stare met hers and he nodded. "Hurry."

18

Hayden swayed on her feet as she blinked away a couple more tears. It was strange to grieve for someone she'd only properly met as they were taking their final breaths. After Austin's storytelling, the people on the ranch seemed sort of like celebrities to her. She knew all about them, but they had no clue who she was. Even if they had been strangers, it would have been impossible to remain unfazed by the outpouring of sorrow from everyone surrounding her when her own emotions were so ragged and close to the surface.

She swore she'd cried more in the past few days than in the rest of her life combined. At least with her new medicines, she wasn't experiencing the stabbing pain in her side she'd come to associate with stressful situations.

"You must be exhausted." Austin came up behind her and wrapped his arms around her waist as they watched the coroner drive away after interviewing them and handling Jake's body. She wasn't sure if he was comforting her or drawing strength from her when he kissed the top of her head then rested his chin there. Maybe both. "Do you still have your key to my place?"

"I'm not leaving without you." She spun in his arms then and hugged him tight. It was only right to give him what comfort she could in his time of need. After all, he'd been there for her in hers.

Austin's father, Silas, must have overheard them. He approached and said, "There's nothing else you can do here. Take her home. Be careful if you talk to your cousins. No one has been able to reach James yet."

Oh God. Hayden hadn't even thought of that. It would be devastating to break the news to them. At least she could be there with Austin if he had to deal that blow to his best friend.

"Thank you. Jake's greatest fear was dying alone. Because of you, he didn't have to," Silas said to her before someone dragged him away to attend to one of a million other important things happening in the aftermath of Jake's death. She didn't even have a chance to respond.

At that point both she and Austin seemed incapable of reacting normally. They really did need to get out of there and chill out.

"Ever ride a horse before?" Austin wondered.

"Nope."

"Then you can double up with me. I won't let you fall." He led her to a stall. The horse there lifted its head and huffed out a breath almost as if it was greeting him. "This is Aubrey."

"That's an unusual name for a horse, isn't it?"

He shrugged. "Honestly, I think it was some kind of inside joke. Who knows around here? Anyway... He's really gentle, don't worry."

With Austin to keep her safe, she wasn't concerned in the least. In fact, if it wouldn't result in her broken neck, a full-speed gallop sounded more cathartic at the moment. It disturbed her more to hear the inconsolable sobbing coming from a few stalls down where Austin's aunt Cindy and uncle Sam mourned together over the loss of their friend while Austin saddled the horse. Hayden wondered what stories Austin might have left out about the pair of them and Jake. His loss seemed to cut them deeper than most. Hayden rubbed her side, impacted by their distress.

"Is it hurting?" Austin seemed poised to throw her over his shoulder and race her back to the emergency room, just in case.

"No. It's okay," she promised. "Just habit."

"I've had enough, too," Austin told her as he finished saddling the horse. "I need to go somewhere quiet for a while. Somewhere you and I can be alone and unwind." He slapped his hat against his thigh.

Hayden wished she knew how to help him relax as he'd done for her repeatedly. The only thing that came to mind—which involved getting naked and very sweaty—might not be a strategy he'd appreciate. The more she thought about it, though, the better of an idea it sounded like.

"Up you go." He curled his fingers, gesturing for her to come closer. When she did, he took her left hand and put it on the horse's withers. "Grab a handful of mane. Put your other hand on the saddle."

She did as he instructed. Up close the docile horse seemed a lot more powerful. It was beautiful.

Austin reached down and tapped her left shin. "Pick up this foot. On the count of three, pull yourself up. I'll give you a boost."

On his signal, she hopped and pulled, but his assist beneath her knee and ankle made her feel like she was flying onto the horse's back. With Austin, everything was easier.

"Great, now scoot behind the saddle." He steadied her while she adjusted her position.

"Do you always have to drive?" she teased as he joined her with a single graceful motion, taking the reins.

"It's kind of my thing, but if you're interested I'm happy to teach you some other time." He glanced over his shoulder, smiling at her. "Wrap your arms around me and hang on. We're going to walk, and he knows this trail by heart, but any animal could always get spooked."

With Austin in control she figured that wasn't very likely. He was an expert at keeping the horses calm and leading them where he wanted them to go. His skills worked on people, too. She should know since he'd put them to good use handling her until he'd gained her trust.

She hugged him, enjoying the freedom to explore the ridges and valleys of his ripped abdomen in the name of safety. Hayden laid her cheek between his shoulders and sighed.

"Ready?" he asked.

"Yup." If he only knew how ready she was. Not only for the trip, like he'd intended.

They were silent as they meandered back to his apartment. The swish of long grass and the rustle of new spring leaves lulled her as they swayed in time to the motion of the horse. The tranquil surroundings countered their lingering anguish.

Wrapped around Austin, it was easy to sense his body relaxing against her bit by bit. Her knotted muscles began to melt, too. Her chest and his back pressed more closely together by the minute.

When they crested a gentle hill and she spotted his barn at the foot of it, she sighed.

"Almost there."

"I'm not in any rush," she murmured. "This is nice. It feels like we're somewhere else, far away from all our problems."

"This week has been...overwhelming. That's for damn sure." He cleared his throat. "It's too much. Every time I think we've turned a corner, something else happens. And that's not a challenge, life. You're welcome to get better instead of worse this time."

For the first time, she saw him being something other than utterly positive. It was her turn to lift him up.

She lost the opportunity to act when he disentangled her arms from around him then dismounted outside his house. He opened the big bay before leading the horse inside with her still on it. Austin put the horse in the single stall at the rear of the building, removed its saddle, and held his arms up to her. She went into them, maybe a little too eagerly.

As he lowered her to the floor, their torsos slid across each other inch by inch.

Hayden trusted her instincts. When he paused with her at eye level, she whispered. "I think I know a way to turn things around."

He hummed and craned his neck to capture her lips with his, accepting her invitation for what it was. Hayden wrapped her thighs around his hips and crossed her legs behind his back. He palmed her ass and began to walk, pausing only to shut the stall door behind them.

They didn't make it far. As she teased him with the tip of her tongue against his lips, he groaned. Austin spun around and pressed her shoulders to his rig. He leaned into her, trapping her between the searing heat of his muscles and the cool metal. For the first time, he wasn't treating her with kid gloves.

And she loved it.

Hayden buried her fingers in his hair, tugging some to encourage his welcome aggression. One of his hands glided up from her ass to her side. He slipped it beneath her shirt and skimmed up her uninjured ribs until his thumb rested right below her breast. Hayden gasped in anticipation, her head rocking backward.

All that did was expose her throat to Austin. He took advantage, kissing and nipping some of the most sensitive parts of her. She arched in his hold, grinding her pelvis against his.

She whimpered when something steely pressed between her thighs. "That's one hell of a belt buckle."

"I'm not wearing one, baby." He chuckled and rocked his hips to make her aware of the full length of his hard-on tucked between her legs.

"Oh fuck," she moaned.

"That's where this is headed if we're not careful." He forced her to meet his stare, which she'd never seen so intense before. His gaze bored into her. "Is that really what you're asking for?"

"Yes." No doubt about it.

"I need to get lost in you. So bad." He sealed his confession with another kiss, this one overflowing with passion and a hint of desperation. She knew exactly how he felt. After realizing her father was gone forever, a sense of urgency had infiltrated her spirit. She didn't want to spend another moment not living her life to the fullest.

Very few things she'd ever experienced had felt as good as this. She craved more.

A lot more.

Austin didn't seem willing to waste any time either. He yanked down the soft turquoise leggings she wore beneath the tunic shirt he'd picked out for her, then slid the crotch of her panties to the side. A moment later, a strangled cry escaped her as he plunged two thick fingers inside her.

It had been so long since she'd been that full. Stars danced in her vision even as her body clamped down on his hand. It hurt some. Joy, pleasure, and relief eclipsed the pain.

He growled as he began to move his fingers within her, spreading her moisture along her channel. His thumb flicked over her clit, drawing more lubrication from her to coat his digits. When he slid easily in and out, he withdrew, leaving her panting.

"You're so hot. So soft." He kissed her again, with greater

urgency. "I can't wait until my cock is buried inside you, being hugged by that pretty pussy."

Whoa. No one had ever talked to Hayden like that. Her arousal spiked. If she didn't find an outlet for the rush of feelings swirling inside her, they would tear her apart. "Do it."

Austin reached into his back pocket and withdrew his wallet. He took a condom from inside and ripped it open with his teeth. He shifted her slightly, just enough to jam his hands between them, yank his zipper down, withdraw his hard-on, and cover himself with the latex before setting the blunt tip of it against the opening to her body.

Nothing had ever felt so right.

"I swear I will make this up to you later." He braced his left forearm on the trailer beside her head and guided himself inside her with his right hand.

At first he seemed stuck barely within her. She cried out his name and clawed his back, stunned by the intensity of their first joining. Every inch she lowered onto his shaft sent a riot of sensation up her spine. She stopped thinking and gave in to instinct.

Austin worked inside her until she swore she couldn't take even a tiny bit more. He packed her completely, took every bit of her emptiness, and made it his.

By the time he began to drill within her—with quick jabs then longer strokes—she could already sense the tightening of her pussy. Each time he tapped her clit with his torso, she spasmed around him.

And when he threaded his hand beneath both her shirt and her bra to squeeze her breast, she knew it wasn't going to take much more to cause her to explode. He pinched her nipple lightly and covered her mouth with his. Austin plundered, sucking on her tongue and never once looking away from her eyes. She saw it then, in his stare. The same frantic yearning she felt.

That was what put her over the edge—knowing he needed her as badly as she needed him.

Hayden screamed and quaked in his arms. She flew into an orgasm so intense she thought she might black out. Just when she was certain she had experienced as much ecstasy as humanly possible, Austin set himself loose on her. He fucked her hard and fast, driving completely within her as she undulated around him.

He bucked and roared. Several grunts echoed through the barn as he poured his lust into the condom he wore then stilled, embedded to the hilt inside her. They couldn't possibly have gotten any closer than they were at that moment, and she wasn't only thinking of their bodies. Loss and fear had leveled them. The bond they were forging could be a foundation to rebuild their lives on.

"Shit, I can't believe I just did that." He wiped his mouth on the back of his hand. "I tried to be so gentle with you. Careful. And then I acted like a savage anyway. I didn't want to be like other guys..."

"If that's what every other guy is like, I've been missing out." She shot him a rueful grin, fully aware he was referring to her ex. "I'm wrecked. That was incredible."

She wanted to do it again. Lots.

Austin leaned his forehead on hers and laughed softly. "Thanks. At least let me take care of you now."

She already felt pretty well spoiled, but she didn't have the strength to argue when he lifted her into his arms and carried her upstairs. In his bedroom, he laid her gently on the plush mattress. Austin toed off his boots, then ripped off his shirt and hooked his thumbs in the waistband of his jeans. When he slipped them off, she realized he was half hard again already.

She licked her lips.

"It's no wonder I lost it down there. I didn't mean to fuck you like a rabid animal." He stripped her as he talked, admiring every part of her that he revealed to his gaze, pausing to kiss and caress along the way. "Especially after what you've been through, I had hoped that if we ever got to this point, I could show you I was better than that."

"How much better could it be?" she wondered rhetorically, and held her arms out to him.

Though she could have easily passed an entire afternoon appreciating his naked form, she'd rather have it tucked against her, keeping her warm.

It seemed he agreed when he slid between the covers and gathered her to him so she draped over his chest like another blanket. Hayden had been transported to a place where emotion ruled over reason. So when her instincts told her to pacify Austin the best way she knew how, she went with it. She kissed him softly, over and over.

She folded her arms on his chest and studied his face as they made out endlessly.

Eventually she needed a break to catch her breath.

"Thank you for staying with me today." He held her tight, stroked down the length of her back from her shoulders to the rise of her ass. In some sick way, it felt amazing to know he'd needed to lean on her like she'd done with him this past week. It sucked that he'd fallen to her level. Yet in that dark moment, she'd felt like his equal.

Which could explain why she acted on the connection that had grown between them every second they spent together. Hayden brushed the hair off his brow lightly then kissed him. It was her turn to take care of him, to give him solace even if that meant surrendering to his affection instead of being the aggressor in bed. Anything that brought him comfort was fair game.

"I didn't intend to take advantage of you and your empathy," he whispered against her lips.

"You're not. *I'm* taking advantage of *you* and your suffering to justify something I've been wanting to do anyway." She owed him the truth about that.

"Oh. Well, that's okay then." The corner of his mouth kicked up slightly. "Seriously, Hayden, I've been dying to show you how a real man treats his woman. Today of all days, it seems like wasting time or finding excuses to withhold your feelings from someone should be a crime. So I'm going to be honest—I think you're an amazing woman. I want you. Bad."

"Take me then. For tonight"—*and maybe every night*, she added silently—"I'm yours."

She sealed her promise with a kiss. It wasn't tentative or innocent.

No, this was a passionate battle cry.

Austin rose to the occasion. He groaned and tunneled his fingers into her hair, flexing them against her scalp until he urged her close enough that he could devour her. Blissed on rejuvenating lust, she squeaked when he rolled, taking her to her back so that he hovered over her on straight-locked arms.

"If you're mine, I can do whatever I want with you, right?" He trailed the tip of his index finger over her swollen lips, making her shiver.

She nodded.

"Good, then lie back and spread your legs." He waited until she obeyed, then pressed the inside of her thigh. "Wider."

Hayden did as told. Austin snaked his way down her body, touching and tasting every patch of skin he passed along the long, winding, very circuitous path he took. He spent forever teasing her and sampling each part of her body. A long while later, his chin nudged her mound. She called out his name.

"Hmm?" He peeked up at her with a grin. "Is there something you want?"

Hayden nodded.

"Ask for it, baby." He pulled back enough to blow softly over her pussy.

"Lick it. Please." Her hand moved to the back of his head, but he wasn't having any of that.

Austin wrapped his fingers around her wrists then held them against the bed, trapping them. It should have terrified her. It didn't.

"Is this okay?" he double-checked anyway.

"I'm dying. Please."

The vibrations from his wicked laugh nearly undid her. Her hips lifted off the bed as she sought deeper contact. He didn't disappoint. Hayden couldn't believe sex like this had been possible her whole life and she'd only had the faintest idea. Embarrassment might have derailed her rapture if Austin hadn't refused to let her be distracted.

He licked, sucked, and rubbed, fingered and ate.

All she could do was enjoy. And she did. Her heels drummed on the bed restlessly as she grew closer to orgasm. Austin redoubled his efforts, refusing to let her retreat from the onslaught of pleasure. He added his fingers to the mix, inserting them into her pussy and curling them so they tapped some secret place even she hadn't known about before.

Hayden screamed as she shattered. She rode his face shamelessly as he wrung drop after drop of arousal from her. When she eventually regained awareness, she expected to return the favor.

Austin shook his head. "I'm not finished with you."

"Hmm?" She couldn't form a more articulate response.

Instead of wasting his energy on talking, Austin began the process of arousing her all over again. And again, and again, and again. She lost count of how many times he made her climax, wringing pleasure from her until she thought she might drown in it.

Only when she begged him for a break did he crawl up her body and smother her with his huge, hard body. He kissed her, sharing the taste of her own arousal merged with the flavor of his lips. His cock sat heavily on her belly as he toyed with her mouth.

Though she would have thought it impossible minutes before, she ached to hold him inside her again. "Austin, please fuck me."

"No, baby." He nuzzled her neck. "There's something I want more. I haven't made love to anyone in a very long time. Not like this. I'm going to bury myself in you, slow and deep. I'm going to ride you as long as I can before I give in to whatever this is between us."

Oh. Well, shit. That sounded good, too.

She put her hands on his hips and tried to steer him into place. Austin grinned. "Don't worry, I'm going to give you all of me. I swear. In fact, unless you have an objection, I'm going in bare. I'm clean and I know you are too since you asked me to stay when you talked with the doctor the other day. And we're both on birth control…"

"Oh God, yes. Do it." And then he was there, answering her prayers. He glided into her with a single persistent penetration that made her eyes roll back in her head. She tried to outlast him, but it was impossible.

"I didn't say anything about you waiting. Go ahead, Hayden. Come for me. Come on me."

Her body obeyed him without pause.

Still he didn't cave. She crested several times before sweat beaded on his brow and his jaw clenched so tight she thought he might crack a tooth.

Austin's hands roamed across her, everywhere he could reach. She mirrored him, stroking his back and grabbing his bunching ass as he sped up almost imperceptibly.

Hayden knew she'd been on the right track last week when she'd thought the safe haven of his trailer had been her salvation. But this, coming apart in his arms as he flooded her with his desire, was truly heaven on earth.

With one last guttural moan, Austin emptied himself into her.

They whispered praise to each other as they cuddled, wallowing in the sheer bliss they'd generated together to salve some of their recent hurts. They spent the rest of the day and the entire night learning all the ways they could make each other feel incredible.

They might not have gotten much sleep, but the next morning Hayden felt rested and refreshed. Prepared to handle the difficult days ahead. Together, they could survive pretty much anything.

Or at least she was foolish enough to think so at the time.

19

____

This wasn't how Hayden would have preferred to meet Austin's family. One by one, they'd all come home. Bryant, Doug, and James—whom they'd finally gotten a hold of—were there, gathered around a bonfire.

The official celebration of Jake's life wasn't scheduled until the following day. Informally, friends and neighbors had come to express their condolences, deliver food, and offer to help the family with preparations. In addition, the ranch hands were idle. Everyone had rare time off with minimal responsibilities until regular operations resumed.

With gobs of people milling around, an impromptu potluck had cropped up and lasted past sundown. A swarm of children, including Austin's adorable nieces and nephews, buzzed around catching fireflies, oblivious to the gravity of the situation.

Austin had ushered her around to officially meet each of the four legendary Compass brothers, starting with his own parents.

"We won't forget that you've stepped up in our family's time of need." Silas took her offered hand and drew her into a crushing embrace. So that's where his son had learned it from.

"Dad, tell him to knock it off. He's making us sound like the mafia or something," Austin groaned to Colby, who only laughed.

"He does what he wants, you know that." Colby let go of their wife's hand as he threw up his own. "Besides, I agree with him. It might have taken you five years to bring a girl home, but you chose wisely."

Hayden loved their closeness and frank, sentimental exchange. It was something she'd never been part of before. When Silas let her breathe again, his hug was followed up by one from Austin's mom and then his dad. "It means a lot that you say that. Thank you. But the only reason I was here in the first place was because Austin was helping me out. You have no idea how much he's done for me. You raised an incredible man."

Lucy hummed as she took in the way Austin was watching her and the fact that his hand rode low on her spine, even now. Her mom-sense had to be going off full force. She knew what was happening here and didn't seem to be too upset about it. In fact, she seemed to nod slightly.

Huh.

"You've obviously had a rough time lately with your medical issues and your father." Lucy kindly didn't mention the black eye and cracked ribs that Austin's uncle Sawyer had insisted on taking a report on. "To be here, still standing, and supporting our son at the same time... Well, you're pretty damn strong, like the rest of the Compass women."

Hayden wished she could call herself one of them permanently. With everything that had been going on, she and Austin hadn't spoken about the future or where she would go from here.

They couldn't evade the topic forever, though.

Soon the fairytale would be over.

Their conversation ended there when Austin's uncles Sam, Sawyer, and Seth joined them, along with their wives. She spent a while talking to each one until Uncle Sawyer pulled her off to the side. "I want you to know I didn't have a chance to follow up on your reports yet. I was poking around, offering to assist on the cold case regarding your father when we got the news about Jake and..."

"That's fine. I understand." She smiled weakly, ashamed to even have to think about Bobby Joe in the presence of Austin's perfect family.

"What I'm saying"—he looked up and included Austin in his statement—"is that you should be careful until I do. I'd recommend going back and filing for a restraining order once the documentation is in place."

Hayden hadn't intended to return. Ever. Disappearing and starting over somewhere new had been her plan all along. "Thank you, I'll consider doing that once I figure out where I'm going from here."

"Going?" Uncle Sawyer tipped his head.

Awkward.

Austin didn't object. But neither did he affirm that she was a temporary resident in his apartment.

"Uh." Uncle Sawyer cleared his throat. "I'll leave you two alone. I just thought I would mention it to be safe."

"I appreciate your help." Hayden stepped forward and hugged him in the Compass tradition. Not before she saw him shoot Austin an unreadable glare over her head. He patted her back gently.

"Anytime."

With that, they were tugged away again. This time by shouts from the rest of the Compass boys, who were harassing Austin to join them by the roaring fire they'd built. James in particular seemed eager to introduce them to a woman named Ivy he'd met as a smokejumper.

She was stunning, with blue eyes that stood out against her dark brown hair. Though she was petite, she was curvy—pretty much every woman's ideal figure. It seemed as though she was a great match for James, anticipating what he was going to say and sitting awfully close to him.

Hayden could understand.

She was content to sit quietly and observe their meet-up so long as Austin was nearby. They were funny, naughty, and ultimately charming.

Austin held her hand and occasionally brushed his thumb over it in between jabs at his cousins and drags on his beer. It was the first time she'd seen him drink, and though she started the night out hyperaware of his every reaction, she soon realized he was nothing like Bobby Joe.

Okay, so she'd already known that.

Lost in her thoughts, she didn't immediately notice when they quieted down. It was the way Bryant tensed across from her that tipped her off to someone approaching.

"Hey, Vaughn." James lifted a hand in greeting. "How's it going?"

"Not the best day in Compton Pass history." A scrappy cowboy with midnight-black hair stepped up to the cooler at their feet to grab a beer out of the ice, then opened it with his teeth like it was nothing. "Otherwise I'm okay. How about you guys?"

Though he spoke to them all, his gaze bored into Bryant when he asked.

"Fine." The usually soft-spoken though friendly cousin turned downright frosty. Interesting.

"Vaughn, this is Hayden." Austin added to Hayden, "He's our resident tattoo artist. He's done a bunch of my ink."

"Good job." She smiled up at him. "I love his tattoos."

Vaughn winked at her. "I do what I can for my clients. Happy to see it's helping him out. Austin's been in need of a good woman for a while—"

Austin cut that shit off right there. He told Bryant, "You should see Hayden's. You'd love it. It's all about water, the ocean, and a ship. Even a quote about water." Hayden didn't blame him either. She didn't need to know about his past conquests.

"Maybe you're with the wrong cousin," Doug teased. His joke didn't hold a lot of weight since it was no secret, nor any big deal to them, that Bryant was gay.

"Smart guys *are* pretty hot." She smiled at him, hoping to erase some of the unease she sensed building within him. "I hear you're an environmental scientist or will be soon."

"If I ever finish this dissertation." He cursed under his breath. "I need to run a few more experiments while I'm home. Maybe even come back for a few months to work on some additional support for my thesis."

Although no one had asked his opinion, Vaughn chimed in, "Maybe your problem is that you work too much, Bryant. Always did. I remember Jake telling you lots of times to cut loose and have some fun. In his memory, I'd be willing to help you out with that."

Well, dammmmmmmn. Hayden's eyes grew as big as tractor tires as her gaze ping-ponged between the two men. It was clear to her in that instant that there was some history there, or maybe there could have been. Thinking about the two powerful, well-muscled sexy beasts like them clashing in bed had her so hot she might need to plunge her whole head in that ice bucket to keep from combusting.

"You know I don't date cowboys." Bryant sounded as though he might need a dunk or two of his own. A full out ice bath might not be out of the question.

"Always thought that was a stupid rule," the man practically snarled. "I know you had another one about no tattoos. If you decide to break either, you know where to find me. I've got the equipment that did your parents' ink and the skill to use it."

"Hang on." Austin grabbed Vaughn's arm and swung him back around before he could bail on them. "You mean that? Snake gave it to you? I didn't know that."

The guy shook off Austin's grip but nodded. "Yeah. Another Compass legend, that guy. I miss his bony ass. He taught me everything I know."

"I used to tease Jake about getting a tattoo of him. He fucking *hated* that idea." Austin lit up. Hayden knew him well enough now to know he'd already decided to do it. "Can I come see you sometime soon to make that happen? I have a few other ideas, too. Maybe a portrait of my parents and Jake over a landscape with my truck driving over a road that leads all across the earth. And a compass in there somewhere, of course."

"Do you have any room left?" Vaughn looked Austin up and down. "You'd need a helluva lot for all that."

"Saved my whole back for something important. For this." He nodded.

"Sounds good. Come by next week, whenever you're free. My new shop is open every night except Thursdays. Bring your cousin—the sexy one—and I'll give you a discount." He saluted them with his beer bottle before vanishing into the evening and the crowd lingering beyond the light from the flames.

Everyone stared at Bryant.

"What? I'm not interested, okay?" He scrubbed his hands over his face.

"This is exactly why you're going to regain your virgin status soon." James knocked back another swig of something potent. It made Hayden a little nervous, but he didn't seem to lose control like Bobby Joe inevitably had.

"Hell, if a guy looked at me like that even *I* might be willing to give it a try." Doug laughed. "Damn, cuz. I think you're missing out."

When Bryant didn't joke back, they let it drop. Hayden slid her hand across the gap between them and squeezed his knee under the cover of the flickering shadows. He turned his head and smiled sadly at her. What was up with that?

The rest of the night passed in a blur as the cousins tried to one-up each other by telling her the wildest stories about their childhood and Austin.

Their sisters left first, needing to put their kids to bed. The Compass Boys harassed them, calling them old ladies. Hayden suspected they were glad to go home to enjoy the private company of their husbands. The rest of their friends and neighbors went next. Eventually it was just the five of them left, hanging out until the fire died and all the beers were empty.

James made sure to douse the embers with the ice water even though the flames had been well contained by a thick ring of rocks. His job as a smoke jumper probably had something to do with that.

"Ready to go home?" Austin asked.

God, she loved the way that sounded. It might not be for real, but for tonight she needed to pretend everything was like it seemed. Either way, she was pretty sure bedtime wouldn't be for a while yet.

"Very." She looped her arms around his neck and drew him down for a kiss. She only meant it to be a quick peck, but it quickly spiraled out of control. When Austin's hand roamed lower and cupped her ass, he drew her pelvis to his so she couldn't mistake the stiff cock he had waiting for her.

Whistling and catcalls from the rest of the Compass Boys broke her from the moment.

"Time to go," Austin told her, then said goodnight to his cousins.

"So I guess we're not crashing at your place?" Doug asked with a mischievous smirk.

"Not unless you brought earplugs," Austin shot back.

Hayden didn't even mind them discussing her sex life when she saw the shit-eating grin on her lover's face. If she had any say, he'd always wear it because of her.

"Have fun, kids." Bryant shooed them.

"We will. Night." She waved and pretended to drag Austin away.

Doug and James laughed, but she caught a heartrending and wistful stare from Bryant before he turned his back on them as if it hurt too much to watch a couple in full-blown...lust.

20

———

Hayden wasn't sure what she'd expected, but Jake's funeral was nothing like she'd imagined. In fact, it wasn't really a funeral at all. Having lived through two major Compass Ranch send-offs for first JD and then Vicky Compton, he'd always said he'd rather something informal and nontraditional.

Years ago, he'd told Viho he'd like it if anyone who cared to join them came together and shared their favorite memories of him when it was his time. Though it was obviously a struggle for the people closest to him, like Viho, Cindy, Sam, and his grandchildren, they did their best to honor his wishes and celebrate his life.

Jake's ashes were in a polished wooden box carved from the limb of a tree that grew over Viho's mom's grave. It sat on a table in the middle of the living room of the main ranch house.

People came and went, leaving a memory or learning something new about the man they'd all revered. While others continued to share, Hayden got up to use the restroom and took her time returning. She wandered through the old farmhouse,

155

running her fingers over the chair rail molding that led down the hallway and into the formal dining room.

She got the feeling no one ever used this space, preferring instead to share meals in the kitchen and living room as they were today. This part of the house seemed untouched by renovations. It was easy to imagine the happy couple hanging near Austin's stove living here. The love they'd shared in this place had left permanent marks.

In the laughter and tears of their descendants, which echoed off the walls surrounding them, she could still feel their spirits. Two people had been at the root of all this. Their passion had been powerful enough to make a lasting difference in the world.

Austin's own parents were doing their damnedest to continue that tradition. They'd moved into the main house and raised their own children to be compassionate, loving, fiery people. What would her own life have been like if she'd grown up in a home like this, with a family as exceptional as the Comptons?

Though she couldn't change the past, Hayden swore then and there that was her goal for her future—to build an empire of devotion and affection that would last for generations. Whether that was by herself or with a man like Austin down the road, when she was ready for that possibility once more, she couldn't say.

Hayden sat on the piano bench and wished she knew how to play.

"You okay?" Leah stood in the doorway.

"Hi. I'm fine." Hayden nodded, surprised to realize for the first time in a long time, she kind of was. Day by day she was getting stronger, healing up from Bobby Joe and her ulcers, and falling harder for Austin.

Uh oh. That wasn't a good thing, was it?

It meant she'd run out of reasons to take shelter at his place. She'd never meant to stay even this long. And now she was attached to him, his family, and his home. That would be fine if they'd met under different circumstances. But Hayden needed to go out on her own soon. She'd been trapped with Bobby Joe because she'd never learned to make it solo.

That had to change or she'd never be able to be happy in a relationship.

She didn't intend to be a burden for someone, requiring constant care. She needed to be an equal partner. Which meant her time at Compass Ranch was coming to an end.

"I'm not so sure about that. But I think I have something that might help," Leah said as she came closer. Which was when Hayden noticed the embossed leather guitar case she carried. "This guitar was my best friend for a while. I've played it at weddings and funerals in this family. But I haven't sat down with it very much in years and neither my daughter nor any of the other kids are interested in learning."

Hayden's fingers itched to hold the instrument. "Did you bring it today so I could perform a song? I don't have any stories to share, but I'd be glad to do this for Jake."

"While I'd love to hear you play it, that's not why I brought it." Leah sat on the bench next to her. She laid the case across their laps, then opened the lid. The gorgeous acoustic guitar inside took Hayden's breath away. If it sounded even half as good as it looked, it would be incredible. Mother of pearl flowers and butterflies decorated the entire body and continued up the neck. She sighed as she traced one of the swirls along the polished wood. Gorgeous. "It needs a new home."

Hayden perked up at that. Could she be that lucky? "I have about five hundred dollars. I realize this case alone is worth more than that, but if I could use it to get a few paying gigs, I could set up a payment plan. How much is fair?"

She worried an heirloom-quality instrument like this would be so far out of her reach as to be laughable. An unattainable dream like a lot of the other things at Compass Ranch.

"It's not for sale," Leah was quick to correct her, closing the lid and latching it once more.

"Oh, I'm sorry. I misunderstood."

"Yes, you did." Leah hugged her, then held the case out to Hayden. "It's already yours. There have been times in my life when just the right thing happened at just the right moment. This is one of them. I feel like it was meant to be."

Hayden wondered if there'd be a single day she spent with the Comptons that she didn't end up in tears. She used her index fingers to wipe droplets from the corners of her eyes. "I'm so lucky to have met you all. I will never forget this."

"Someday, when you can, do something for someone else. That's pretty much how we operate around here."

Hayden nodded and whispered, "Thank you."

From the living room, the drone of the TV that had been playing in the background got louder, drawing their attention. Especially when an oddly familiar voice lifted every single hair on the back of Hayden's neck.

What the hell?

"Hayden! You'd better come in here!" someone—Doug, she thought—yelled.

As her insides tried to twist in their usual cramp, she darted for the other room and the TV, hoping she would be in time to turn it off and keep the entire Compass clan from witnessing her dirty laundry being aired across the nation.

Nope. No chance of that.

Because there on the screen was the biggest bunch of bullshit she'd ever seen.

"If you've seen her, please tell her I love her and I'm sorry. I just want to know that she's safe," Bobby Joe cried for the cameras, probably wondering if he'd killed her and buried her body in the woods before he'd blacked out. He held up an outdated picture of her from their high school yearbook. The fact that he hadn't been able to find something more recent spoke volumes.

She flinched when Austin cursed violently from beside her.

A headline stamped across the bottom of the screen read *Manhunt underway for missing waitress.*

"Hayden's not missing, she's right here." One of Austin's nieces pointed helpfully to her before Sterling could shush the girl. "I found her! Yay!"

Austin latched onto her hand, gripping it tight, as though she might evade him and fly from the ranch like she wished she could. He led her out onto the porch where a bench swing would have tempted her to sit if the situation had been different.

"I have to go back," she blurted as soon as they were alone.

"I know."

"You do?" He wasn't going to stop her? Thank God.

"Of course. And I'm going with you." He spread his booted feet as if bracing for a fight.

As he should have. "You've done enough. I'm not getting you any more tangled up in this mess than you already are."

"You're not going alone. I've seen what that piece of shit is capable of. And I think you got lucky escaping with just a few bruises." He crossed his arms. "I have a few things I'd like to say to good old Bobby Joe."

"Definitely not." He might be bigger than Hayden, but she was done with bending. For anyone.

"You don't believe what he was spouting off to the media, do you? Are you hoping to get back together with him?" Austin grew very still and quiet.

"Hell no!" Hayden clutched her new guitar and suddenly

she knew what she had to do. "But I need to file those reports against him. Get the restraining order like your uncle told me to. I need a clean break so I can start over without these problems haunting me."

Austin took a step closer to her.

She stepped back. "And I need to do it alone."

21

———

Austin watched her disappear into the night with only the clothes on her back and his aunt Leah's guitar. At least she had more than she did when he'd discovered her stealing his damn jacket. She'd insisted on walking alone to his house to pick up her cash and the little suitcase with the rest of her belongings.

By the time he got home, she'd be gone from his life.

Reeling, he stumbled back inside his parents' house. Bryant was sitting on the steps to the upper story, just inside the back door. "You didn't actually let her leave, did you?"

"What choice do I have? She wants to go." Austin shrugged and tugged on his hair. "Besides, the family needs me."

"She needs you more." Bryant got up and smacked Austin on the back of the head.

"What the—?"

"That was for Jake. Don't want the guy to have to come back from the dead to give you another lecture." His cousin glared at him. "I'll tell them where you went. They'll understand. At least until she squares this shit up with that loser, you can't leave her unprotected. Will you be able to forgive yourself if something happens to her?"

Torn, Austin stared toward the kitchen, then out into the gathering darkness. "No, of course not."

"Then you better start running, dumbass," Bryant told him.

Austin's father emerged from the shadows then, Colby at his side. Silas said, "Listen to him, son. He is the smart one in the family. Go get your girl. Don't let her do this alone."

"But don't make her feel like she *couldn't* do it alone, if she really wanted to," Colby added. "Deep down, no one wants to handle shit like this by themselves, but they need to know they could if they had to."

His mom came from behind the men then and hugged Austin tight. "I like her. And I think you really like her. She could be the one for you. Don't screw up now. Go."

Austin couldn't speak. He didn't have to. He hugged his mom then dashed out the door, careful not to break the family's cardinal rule and let it slam behind him. He sprinted down the dirt path toward his house, in the direction Hayden had taken off in.

He started to wonder if she'd veered off the trail when he caught a flash of her dress through the trees. "Hayden, wait!"

She didn't stop for a second.

It took him a few minutes but he caught up before she could slip through his fingers and out of his life. "Hayden, listen. I'm not trying to fight your battles for you, okay?"

"You're not?" She paused, causing him to nearly plow into her.

He put his hands out to catch her shoulders. "No. Just think this through. He's hurt you before. Let me take you back. I'll stay while you do what you have to do and then—once it's safe —if you want me to leave, I will."

"And you're not going to pick a fight that would land you in trouble? Or even talk to him, for that matter? There's nothing you could say that would make a difference to him."

Oh, but Austin had a lot to get off his chest. He clenched his teeth and drew a breath through his nose. Eventually, he compromised. It was that or nothing. "Fine. I won't interfere in any way as long as you don't go alone. Moral support only. And maybe some road head on the way. Pinky swear."

She didn't respond, but her hand rubbed her side where her ribs still proved he wasn't exaggerating about the danger she could be in.

"Bring me with you. With my uncle's help, we'll clear things up quickly, file for a restraining order, and you can move on with your life for good."

"Okay."

"He's not going to lay another—" Austin paused. "Wait. Did you say okay? As in you'll let me stay with you?"

"A little longer."

"I'll take it." He wrapped her in his arms and stole a quick kiss, nothing like the one he wanted to give her. But it would do for now.

"I'm sorry to do this to you. The timing is shit. Are you sure?" She didn't shove him away, so he stroked her hair, alarmed to feel her trembling beneath his caresses.

"I don't mean to be crass, but Jake isn't coming home. There's no reason not to do what has to be done right away. Besides, he wouldn't think much of me if I didn't take care of you."

"I can take care of myself. Mostly."

Austin held his hands up, palms out. "I don't doubt that. But it never hurts to have backup, right?"

She nodded. "Let's go."

22

"**I** wasn't serious about the road head thing," Austin rasped as he concentrated on keeping them on the highway and in their lane. "Holy fuck."

"Does that mean you didn't enjoy it?" Hayden's wicked grin as she licked her lips and buckled herself back into the passenger seat of his rig guaranteed she knew exactly how much he had.

Driving his truck would never be the same. Every time he sat here, he'd remember her going down on him and how she'd nearly sucked him inside out. "Damn, baby."

"My favorite part was when you accidentally blew the horn as you came." She laughed then, clutching her stomach. To see her do it out of joy instead of pain touched something in him. Something more important than his dick.

She made his days on the road even more enjoyable. And his nights... *Jesus.*

Austin imagined what it would be like if all his trips were as fun as this one or their previous ride together. He'd brought another load of calves for their customer, who'd snapped up the discount they'd offered since he was heading this direction

165

anyway. While he was in his element, speeding across the earth, Hayden's spark faded the closer they got to her town and her old life.

Her foot tapped incessantly and she fiddled with her hair so much he was afraid clumps might start to fall out.

"Hey, it's going to be okay." He held out his hand, but she didn't grab it right away like usual. What was up with that?

"Is it?" she asked without meeting his gaze.

"Yeah. Uncle Sawyer alerted the police. They called off the manhunt, transferred his reports, and have your papers ready to sign and file. It'll be a quick formality to get this taken care of. I'll be with you the whole time."

"And then what?"

"What do you mean?" he asked, feeling as dense as he had back in his short-lived college career. "You're covered for five years at least. More if you decide to press charges for battery, I'd guess. I'm not a lawyer or anything. We can find one to ask."

She bit her lip and squeezed the bridge of her nose between her thumb and index finger. "Never mind."

Unsure of how else to settle her nerves, he asked, "You want to listen to the radio?"

"Sure." She scanned channels until she found something she liked. It freaked him out that every song she sang along to was a sad one, but he didn't know what to do about it.

Before he could figure it out, they were there—pulling into the parking lot of the small municipal building that housed her local police department. At least part of what he'd promised her came true. They were in and out in less than a half hour.

Austin held the door for Hayden, who read and reread the paperwork in her hand as they exited through the back door into the parking lot.

"Well, look who it is."

"Bobby Joe! What the hell are you doing here?" Hayden

waved her temporary restraining order in his face. "I literally *just* got this and you're already violating it. Are you that stupid?"

"You know Buck hangs out with us and Cletus. Did you think he wasn't going to let it slip you were coming in and why after I made such a fool of myself for you?" Bobby Joe came closer. "I think I deserve an explanation before you vanish again. That ain't asking for much."

Austin angled his chest so that he stood between them. He burned the dirty cop's name into his memory so Uncle Sawyer could handle that fucker through official channels. If anything happened to Hayden—and it wouldn't on Austin's watch—that piece of shit would go down for it as hard as Bobby Joe himself.

"Who the hell is this?" Hayden's ex jerked his chin in Austin's direction. "Is that why you left? Because you shacked up with one of those guys you were selling yourself to at the diner? Some sleazy trucker passing through town?"

Hayden's jaw dropped. "You don't actually believe that bullshit you cooked up, do you?"

Austin had only known her a week and a half, but he didn't. Not for a fucking minute.

"It doesn't matter, Hayden. We both fucked up. I know I haven't been the best guy I could have been for you. But come home and I'll try harder. We don't have to talk about that stuff again. We can get past it, can't we? I...uh...still love you."

Austin jumped into the fray. "Real men don't beat people they love." He couldn't stand to listen to this lowlife spout nonsense a single second longer before putting his boot up the guy's ass.

"Hit her? Have I ever laid a hand on you?" Bobby Joe shot Austin the finger as he glared at Hayden. "Tell him that ain't true."

She stared at her feet, maybe remembering how she'd taken off barefoot and half-naked just to escape this bastard. So Austin answered for her. "I guess she got that shiner and the fractured ribs all on her own then. Maybe she fell down stairs you don't have or walked into your fist somehow?"

"Hayden? What's he talking about?" Bobby Joe's skin seemed to turn whiter then. He paused, his face scrunching as if Austin had triggered a wisp of memory. "Is that true? I can't remember that night or a lot of others. Did I do that? Did I hurt you?"

Maybe the guy had some sliver of conscience left after all. At least when he was sober.

"You hurt her in so many ways you can't even begin to understand them all, you dumb motherfucker," Austin snarled, and snapped at his opponent like the leader of a wolf pack.

"Hey, stay out of this." Hayden slapped her palm on his chest. "This isn't your fight."

"The hell it isn't! Anyone who hurts you will answer to me."

Hayden aimed a stare at him. She didn't seem much less horrified than when she'd shot a similar look at Bobby Joe a few moments earlier. What the hell was going on here?

"You know what, you can keep her." Bobby Joe started backing away when he realized there wasn't any way he was going to win this one. Then he turned to Hayden. "I kind of thought for a while that you wised up. That you left my ass to strike out on your own. I probably wouldn't have blamed you much. I ain't much of a prize anymore. But this... You're dumber than I thought. Making the same mistakes again."

"I think you should worry about getting help for yourself instead of trying to fix my problems. If you don't change soon, it's going to be too late." What he said had to have stung, but Hayden seemed genuine in her last-ditch effort. Austin could see she had loved this worthless sack of shit once. Some part of her might still. That wasn't always enough to make things work between two people, though.

That thought hit him like a kick to the balls.

Bobby Joe spit on the ground at Hayden's feet. "Don't act so high and mighty. You've been with me since you were a kid and now you've already found another guy to stick to like glue. You'll never be strong enough to stand on your own. You weren't made to survive by yourself. So you'll always be trapped. Easy to control."

Austin had had about enough of this. He lunged toward Bobby Joe, only to be drawn up by the pressure of his collar around his neck as Hayden grabbed fistfuls of the back of his shirt when he passed her. "Stop it!" The terror and outrage in her scream halted him in his tracks.

Bobby Joe hastened his retreat, striding for the white truck with dealer plates parked nearby. He shot them a double middle finger this time. "Hope you have a nice fucking life."

Though Hayden watched until he'd peeled out of the lot, kicking gravel and dust in their faces, she didn't say a single thing until Bobby Joe had disappeared down the street.

"You should have let me kick his ass," Austin grumbled.

"Seriously? Do you really think I would *like* being with the kind of guy who resorts to violence after what happened between me and Bobby Joe?" She tossed up her hands then let them fall, her paperwork crunching against her hip.

"The kind of guy who can protect you if necessary? The kind who'd stick up for you, or his sisters, or any person being threatened by a bully like your piece-of-shit ex? Maybe you should." Austin encroached on her personal space, trapping her between his ripped, tattooed chest and the wall.

She looked like she wanted to argue but couldn't. She looked away from him, her cheeks red.

He cupped her face in his hands and swung it back gently. "I'd never hurt you, Hayden."

Then he let go of her and put some space between them.

"I don't want to fight with you." She took a deep breath, closed her eyes, then approached him.

He held his arms open to her and she stepped into them for a loose though lingering hug.

She nearly knocked him on his ass when she said, "But I have to go."

"Where?" He held her shoulders at arm's length, staring into her wide eyes and begging her silently to change her mind.

"Anywhere but here."

"Compass Ranch?"

Hayden winced. "No. Bobby Joe was right about one thing —I need to do this myself. I'm no good to you or anyone else until I can be comfortable on my own first."

"It's not safe—"

"The bus station is right across the street." She pointed at the flickering sign. "I've got my guitar, the clothes you bought me, my little nest egg, and the restraining order—although you can see it means nothing here. I've got to move on. Stick to my original plan to build something for myself. I'll go in and buy the ticket for the very next bus out of here, wherever it's headed."

What right did Austin have to tell her she couldn't? None.

He considered doing it anyway but given her reaction to him fighting for her, he knew it would only alienate her further. So he cleared his throat and said, "If that's what you want."

"It's what I *need* to do. Have a safe trip home. Thanks again for....everything. Meeting you, and your family, changed my life."

Austin couldn't explain how much the same went for him. It would be so weird not to have her beside him anymore. In a short time, she'd become part of his everyday existence. A part he was desperately going to miss.

He did his best to show her that with one final, sweet kiss that went on long enough he thought he might have convinced her. Still, she made no move to join him in the cab.

"I'm dropping these calves off at our buyer before I head

back." He put his hat on his head. "I'll stay overnight there again. You have my number if you change your mind. Or you could just hop in the trailer while I'm sleeping and surprise me by popping out mostly naked at some random gas station."

She laughed sadly then flashed him a soft smile. It didn't stop her from collecting her belongings and waving goodbye. Although Hayden glanced over her shoulder every few steps she took away from him, she never called.

And definitely did not stay a little longer or stow away for the ride.

More than the trailer felt empty on his return journey to Compass Ranch.

23

——————

TWO MONTHS LATER

Austin should have kept driving for another hour at least. Instead, he exited the highway at the Crispy Biscuit. If nothing else, it was familiar when he felt lost. And fine, it reminded him of Hayden.

He parked his truck then slumped forward, resting his forehead on the steering wheel as he attempted to give enough of a shit to get out and complete his checks before calling it a day. He had never been so exhausted or unmotivated in his life. Bryant, Doug, and James tried to convince him it was a lack of sex screwing with his testosterone levels or some shit. Though Austin was about to join Bryant as a card-carrying member of the born-again virgin club, he knew that wasn't his problem.

His life of freedom and independence felt kind of hypocritical now that he wished, every day, Hayden had chosen something else for herself. Something that would benefit him.

It was the misery of those two competing parts of himself playing tug of war with his thoughts and feelings every minute of the day that had exhausted him and drowned him in misery. He couldn't take anymore.

173

His cousins were right. He needed a distraction. To get back on the proverbial horse.

Some sick part of him wondered if this would be the night he finally caved in to Regina's aggressive attempts at seduction. Something mindless and a little ruthless was exactly what he needed to scrub Hayden's sweetness from his memory once and for all.

When Austin stepped inside the bar, he knew immediately that the night wasn't going to go like he'd imagined only moments earlier.

Because up there on the stage where she belonged, was Hayden, strumming his aunt Leah's prized guitar and singing her heart out. With her eyes closed, her face relaxed and open, she poured her own powerful emotions into lyrics that expressed her longing, determination, heartache, and more.

Austin could attest that was smarter than bottling them up inside.

He plopped into a seat with an unobstructed view of the stage despite how far it was from the bar where he usually sat. Despite that, it didn't take long for Regina to spot him and approach.

"Can I get you something, handsome?" she asked without getting handsy or slinging any innuendo. She looked different tonight. Toned down, her hair and makeup seemed more natural and definitely more appealing to him. If Hayden hadn't been in the room, reminding him of how gorgeous she was even if he couldn't have her, he might have told Regina so, too.

She waited patiently to take his order. The only thing he was hungry for wasn't on the menu. "Thanks, but I'll pass on food."

"Something to drink? Or are you just waiting for Hayden to finish up?" Regina asked with a surprising lack of cattiness.

"What? No. She doesn't even know I'm here." He supposed

he should buy something so Charlie could afford to keep paying Hayden well. "I'll take a Coke, please."

"Wow. She got you that bad, huh?" Regina smiled. "I don't know what it is about that girl, but every damn man that comes in here starts drooling over her. She's been giving me some pointers."

"I can tell." Austin smiled, feeling kind of like a jerk for the way he'd thought of her in the past.

For the next hour and a half he nursed his soda. Even the sugar rush had nothing on how Hayden affected his system. He could have watched her sing forever. Except before he was ready, her show was over.

Austin drew the brim of his hat down, tucked his chin to his chest, and wormed through the crowd to put a fat tip in Hayden's jar. Well deserved. He'd only made it a few feet away when she called out to him. "Wait! Where are you going?"

He kept moving, hoping she'd assume she'd mistaken someone else for him.

"I know those tattoos, Austin." She ran after him and put her hand on his arm, making him jerk as shockwaves of instant lust buzzed through him. "Weren't you going to say hello?"

"It would be kind of a dick move to make things awkward for you at your job." Austin shoved his hands in his pockets to keep from grabbing her and stuffing his tongue down her throat. That might make an impression, but it would probably also get him slapped.

"Nah, it's no problem." She grinned. "You know, Regina's actually not so bad. She's just...misunderstood. She's been pretty nice to me when I play here."

"I actually meant that I figured you didn't have any interest in talking to *me* since you never reached out."

"Oh." She rubbed her side, a habit that obviously hadn't gone away though she seemed healthier, her curves fuller and her skin less pale. In fact, she seemed to glow. Her new life agreed with her. "I thought about it. It just didn't seem like a good idea."

"Because...?"

"Because it would have been too easy to let you talk me into coming back than staying just a little longer and a little longer." She put her hand on her hip, daring him to deny it.

"Busted." He shrugged. "That only makes me smart, right?"

"And a little sneaky."

"Hey, honey, you need to fatten this boy up. I think he's lost some weight since last time he was in and he didn't let me bring him anything to eat tonight." Regina smacked his ass as she ratted him out, then flew past with a tray full of orders. He supposed he deserved that.

Hayden cracked up, but sobered fast when she scanned him from head to toe. "You know, she's right. It looks like you've lost what I gained. Are you okay?"

Hell no. He wasn't fucking okay. Was she nuts?

Wait, was she okay without him?

Seemed like it.

"I think I'm going to head out. Been a long day." He rubbed the back of his neck, then spun around.

"It was really...nice...to see you!" Hayden shouted over the packed room as he put some distance between them.

"You too." He didn't bother to turn around as he admitted it.

She had no clue how infatuated he was with her and he'd like to keep it that way, since they were doomed to be separated.

Austin crashed through the front door and staggered to his truck as if he'd slammed an entire fifth of something cheap and strong. It was Hayden. She was intoxicating and slightly poisonous if he let himself get carried away only to have to go through withdrawals again. He face-planted onto his bunk fully dressed and prayed exhaustion would lead him into dreams of the time they'd spent together soon.

So he jolted when, sometime later, someone rapped three times on the passenger side window of his rig.

He initially ignored it, figuring it was Regina, who definitely would not satisfy him tonight despite her recent metamorphosis and didn't deserve to be used like that even if she could. Until he heard Hayden's soft call, "Hey, are you still awake?"

Though he shouldn't have gotten out of bed for her any more than Regina, since neither was good for him in the long run, he couldn't stop himself.

Austin rose and unlocked the door. He cracked it open. Steam rose in front of Hayden from two takeout boxes she held up for him to see. "I owe you dinner. Mind if I come in and eat with you?"

His stomach growled, though whether it was in appreciation of the savory scent of her offering or for the woman herself, he couldn't say. "Sure."

He extended his hand to help her up and nearly cursed at the feel of her silky skin on his.

Despite the gap in their communications, they picked up right where they'd left off. Hayden eagerly told him about how she'd been keeping busy and the progress she was making in establishing herself. Austin updated her on the ranch and his cousins. He carefully edited out any mention of his own misery lately.

Still, she must have sensed something was off.

Engaged in their conversation, he didn't realize they'd both finished their food some time ago until Hayden threw away her trash and crossed to where he sat on the edge of his bunk. She stood between his spread knees and looped her arms around his neck. Her fingers fanned out over the back of his head, which she massaged gently.

"What's really going on with you?" She frowned. "You look like shit."

"Thanks."

She laughed softly then kissed him. It was just a peck, a closed-mouth brush of her lips on his. And it was enough to set him on fire.

Without thinking of the consequences, he leaned in and deepened the contact. Next thing he knew, she was in his lap, her knees planted on the mattress to either side of his thighs. She whimpered and ground herself against his obvious erection.

"This is a terrible idea," Austin said.

"I know."

He groaned. "I want to do it anyway."

"Me too." She grabbed the hem of her shirt then lifted her arms, whipping the soft cotton from her frame with a single, graceful move. It fell to the floor, forgotten.

He unhooked her bra fast enough to get a ticket, then peeled lilac lace from her before he buried his face in her tits. They definitely seemed fuller since the last time he'd had the pleasure of sucking on them. "Damn."

"As much as I enjoy when you draw things out, please don't torture me," she whispered between frantic kisses. "I need you. Now."

Good thing, since he wouldn't have been able to take his time, even if she'd begged.

"Get those jeans off," he ordered as he set about unbuttoning his plaid shirt and unbuckling his belt.

Hayden was gloriously naked the next time he looked up. She looked amazing, even more beautiful than before, with the last hints of trauma erased from her body. Her ass would now make perfect handfuls for him to squeeze or spank while they fucked.

"Come here." He crab-walked backward until he was fully laid out in bed.

She followed him down. Though he wanted to spend all

night kissing her, their tongues sparring, teeth nipping, and mouths gliding across one another, it wasn't very long before making out wasn't enough to satisfy either of them.

Instead of pressing her back and looming over her, pounding into her as he had plenty of times before, he rolled to his back and helped her straddle his hips. "This is all you. Take what you want. Ride me, baby."

Maybe if he handed her the reins, she would realize he wasn't trying to hold her back or tie her down. All he wanted was to share the adventure with her.

She braced herself with her palms on his chest and told him exactly what she craved. "Put your cock in me. I can't wait to hold all of you again, to feel you inside me, stretching me."

Fuck yeah. They'd be lucky if he didn't shoot his load all over her stomach if she kept talking like that. Her newfound confidence ratcheted up his already insane attraction to her.

Maybe she'd been taking lessons from Regina, too.

He reached between them and aimed his dick so that their bodies aligned perfectly.

Then she descended, sheathing him with her soaking wet, hot-as-fuck pussy.

Unleashed, she was spectacular. He saw a side of her that she hadn't fully embraced before, and he fucking loved it. Hayden moaned as she worked him inside her with quick flicks of her hips. While she was busy taking care of that, he touched every part of her on display for him alone. He cupped her breasts and brushed his thumbs over her tight nipples, stroked her belly, and teased her clit, studying the subtle differences in her shape since the last time he'd held her.

When she slid the final bit down his length and captured him entirely within her, they paused and locked stares. It felt so right, he didn't understand how it couldn't be perfect for them both. Not only in that moment, but in the morning as well.

He gripped her hips, encouraging her to fuck.

So she did.

Austin planted his feet on the mattress, and bent his knees so he could assist by spearing up into her even as she ground down on him. It wouldn't have been possible to join themselves any more completely than they were at that moment.

He matched his pace to hers, cursing when she began a sinful figure eight swing of her hips that simultaneously rubbed her clit on his body and did spectacular things to his balls, which were now coated with her arousal.

"I'm getting close," she warned him unnecessarily. The gradual narrowing of her channel, which squeezed his cock, was notice enough.

"Shit, yeah." He redoubled his own efforts, pumping up into her as she met him more than halfway. "Come on me, Hayden. Let me see how much you missed my cock."

She threw her head back, making her long hair sweep over his thighs. The reminder of her gentler side mixed with this new vixen side destroyed him. He tried to hold on, but couldn't.

Luckily she was right there with him.

Austin knew when she came because her pussy clamped around him with rhythmic spasms that accompanied his own orgasm, drawing every jet of his release deeper within her.

Oh yeah, and because she screamed his name loud enough for anyone within a two-state radius to hear. He couldn't say he minded that everyone around knew how thoroughly they could please each other.

"Damn girl, get it!" Regina shouted from outside before her laughter mingled with deeper chuckles filtered through the rig's walls.

Hayden didn't seem to notice. She jerked and trembled above him as she wrung every bit of ecstasy possible from his dick.

When he'd finally finished flooding her pussy, Austin went limp. She collapsed on top of him, pressing her cheek to the spot where his heart attempted to beat through his chest for her. After they'd managed to catch their breath and his cock slipped free of her hold, he wrapped his arms around Hayden and couldn't stop himself from offering, "Do you want to stay a little longer? Spend the night?"

"Would you mind? I was camping in the bus station after shows until Charlie found out. Now he lets me crash in the room over the storeroom out back on the nights I play here, but it's not nearly as comfortable as being in here. With you."

"Hayden..." Austin tried to suppress his protective instincts. She was a big girl, doing what she had to in order to survive.

"I know. It's just for a little while longer, I swear. I've been saving up almost everything I make and looking at used campervans in each town I visit. After riding in here with you, I think it could be fun to have a home on wheels for a while." She kissed his shoulder, then snuggled tight to him with a contented sigh. "For the first time in as long as I can remember, I really am happy, Austin."

"I'm happy *for* you, Hayden." It was the best he could do without lying.

It didn't matter anyway because she didn't hear him. She'd already drifted off to sleep in his arms. He did his best to stay awake and savor the moment, but all too soon the relief from spectacular sex and having her close overwhelmed him.

He slept straight through to morning.

And when he woke, Hayden was already dressed and freshening up.

So much for one more orgasm for the road.

"I have to get going if I'm going to catch my bus." Her smile was rueful when she ambled close enough to straighten his sex-tousled hair. The gentle touches impacted him as deeply as her wild fucking had. "I'm going to miss you."

"I'm only a call or email away." He probably shouldn't have

said that. It would only prolong his suffering without her, but he couldn't give up without trying.

She nodded. "I'll keep that in mind."

Hayden hesitated, then reached into her back pocket for a creased piece of rectangular paper. She handed it to him.

"What's this?" He unfolded it and realized it was a check.

"I tacked on a bit for rent at your place and the food I ate and...well, whatever." She shrugged one shoulder as if it didn't matter, but obviously it did or she wouldn't be bringing it up again when he'd forgotten all about it.

Austin thought of her spending the night on a bench outside a bus station while she scrimped and saved for a better life. He wanted her to reach her goal as quickly as possible.

"I don't want that." He tried to give the check back at the same time she extended her hand to squeeze his. Their fingers collided. He knocked the check out of her hand.

It fluttered to the floor between them.

They both stood there, staring at it. Neither one picked it up.

"You swore to me that you'd take it." The strain in her accusation immediately warned him that he'd fucked up royally. Insulted her and wounded her pride. Told her that he didn't think she was capable when that's not what he'd meant at all.

Son of a bitch! "Hayden..."

"I've got to go, Austin. The bus leaves in twenty minutes. My show tonight is several hours north of here. You'd better go your way, and I'll go mine."

"Stay a little longer and I'll drive you up there."

"Nothing's changed, has it? I'm sorry." She reached up and kissed his cheek before leaving him.

Again.

24

———————

ONE MONTH LATER

"Why are you in such a hurry?" Bryant asked. "What does it matter if you leave with the shipment of hay this afternoon or if you wait until I can ride with you tomorrow morning? I would have thought you'd be up for some company and I need to get the hell away from here for a few days."

Austin kicked the dirt with the toe of his boot.

"Hang on." Bryant caught on. "You're stalking Hayden, aren't you? Are you trying to crash one of her shows tonight?"

"Not exactly. I mean, if I'm going to be in the area anyway, what's the harm in stopping in?" He shrugged as if it wasn't a big deal to compulsively check his ex-lover's new website to see where she was performing and figure out how many miles that was away from him.

"You know, for her, maybe none." Bryant shook head. "But for you, you poor bastard, you're only dragging this out with all your chatting and emails and these hookups that aren't leading anywhere. Let it go. Let *her* go before you really fuck yourself up. Just because you two have insane chemistry doesn't mean that's enough to make it work between you."

Austin glared. "Are you talking about me, or maybe yourself and Vaughn? You think I haven't noticed his truck parked outside of Jake's cabin lately?"

Bryant had been staying there while he was home finishing his research. He cursed. "You could be right, but that only means I know what I'm talking about and I don't want to see you suffer, too."

Austin fisted his hands at his side. "Maybe I just need to try this one last time. If I can't convince her tonight, then at least I'll get to say goodbye properly so I can move on."

"I'll be here when you get home." Bryant smiled sadly. "I'll have a few extra bottles of that nasty whiskey you like ready for celebration or blacking out, whichever is necessary. Hell, I might even drink some with you."

"I appreciate that, cuz." Austin squeezed Bryant's shoulder. "You know you can talk to me about whatever's going on with you two. I've got your back."

Bryant nodded, though tightly. "I don't date cowboys. Especially cowboy tattoo artists."

"But do you fuck them?" Austin wondered, half teasing.

"Apparently they fuck me."

Whoa.

"Well, if he's half as good in bed as he is at work, I'm sure you're in capable hands." Austin diverted slightly when it didn't seem like Bryant planned to elaborate. "The outline for my back piece is nearly finished. Then we just have shading left."

"When can I see it?"

"When it's finished." It wasn't that he was ashamed of what he'd settled on or that he was worried about Bryant's reaction. He just wanted to wait to share until whoever saw it could get the full picture. He'd either made a smart decision or one he would regret.

Tonight would tell him more about that.

Maybe there was still time for Austin to change directions if he quit Hayden for good.

"You'd better get going if you're going to make it before dark." Bryant always gave him his support, even if he didn't think it was wise.

"Say hi to Vaughn for me," Austin said as he tossed in the final bales and secured the trailer. "Tell him I'll be in next Thursday for another session if he's got time."

Bryant nodded, though he left it at that.

25

—————

Austin sat in the shadowy back of a no-name bar in a no-name town. It physically hurt to watch Hayden sing, to hear and see the most beautiful woman in the world and know deep down that hunting season wasn't open. Tonight, like every time they'd bumped into each other—on purpose or by design—since the day at the police station, was going to be all about catch and release.

He was prepared to try one more time before he listened to his cousin's advice and quit torturing himself for his own mental wellbeing.

Ever since he'd encountered her at the Crispy Biscuit and started this chain of hook ups he'd been responding to the emails she'd sent him. Getting to know each other on a deeper level when falling into bed wasn't an option. Though of course they'd had some sexy chats too. He'd also shared more stories about his family when she asked how they were. How could she love them all so much but not want to be part of their clan? Didn't she realize that's what he was offering her? Not only all of himself, but the rest of them, too. They asked about her constantly.

Probably because he'd turned into a lovesick fool.

Hayden was willing to sacrifice not only his affection but that of his family to pursue her career and achieve her independence. If she was that serious, he doubted anything he said would make a difference.

He'd spent an unhealthy amount of time dreaming up schemes to get her back before tossing them in the trash. The reality was, nothing would work until she decided he was good for her. Given her previous disaster of a relationship, she might never believe—as he did—that their bond could elevate them both. It wasn't the kind of dynamic where one of them rose while the other was ground beneath someone's boot.

Mesmerized by Hayden, he didn't quite realize the applause reverberating around him signaled the end of her show instead of a gap between songs. He blinked and she was gone. What the hell?

It took him a second to find her in the dim area around her brightly lit stage. She dodged other patrons as she weaved through the crowd, headed straight for him.

"Hey!" She flung herself into his arms. Of course he caught her. "I wasn't quite sure if that was you. The lights were in my eyes. I'm so glad you're here."

"I—" He bit his tongue to keep from admitting that he'd missed her. "Just happened to be in the area and figured I'd stop by for a bit. You were great. Always are."

"Thanks. I think I'm finding my groove. Have the set list worked out better and I got some sound equipment so I can play some bigger, louder places. I picked up my campervan this morning." She beamed. "It reminds me of being in your rig. I like that."

"I liked that, too." The sight and sound of her naked and coming beneath him as well as the long conversations they'd shared on the road were always in the back of his mind when he drove these days.

"Want to stay a little longer and christen it with me?" She blushed, toying with the top button of his shirt as she asked.

He forced himself to ask the question that could steal an epic night from him. But the more he mulled it over, the more he thought Bryant might have been right. "And in the morning?"

"I'll make sure you're up early enough to head out to your delivery. I've got a gig in the other direction tomorrow night, so I need to move on myself. Don't worry."

She didn't get it at all. That *was* his worry. They kept travelling different directions in life. How could their destinations be the same? He wasn't about to settle for waving and honking or even a quickie each time they crossed paths on the open road. It wasn't enough anymore.

If he couldn't have everything, he couldn't bear to remind himself of what he couldn't keep.

"I'm sorry, Hayden. I can't." He literally could not. It would devastate him to keep letting her go. "I'm so proud of you for making this dream come true. I hope your new life is everything you ever wanted."

That wasn't sarcasm or bitterness seeping through either. He genuinely wished at least one of them was happy. It wasn't going to be him, so it might as well be her.

"Did I say something wrong?" Her brows drew together. "Isn't that why you came tonight?"

He shook his head. "That's not what I was looking for."

"I didn't mean to mislead you. You know how I feel. I thought you were okay with that."

No, it was just that he'd been willing to settle for something, anything, if it meant he could cling to hope for their future. That wasn't her problem. "Hey, you were always honest about being a solo act. No hard feelings. I wish you the best of luck. You deserve to live your dream."

"What's *your* dream?"

"If you're ever ready to settle down again, come back to Compass Ranch and we can figure that out together." He cupped her cheeks between his hands and held her steady as he gave her one final kiss. Hopefully she could feel every bit of his heart, which he poured into it.

"Drive safe, wherever the road takes you," she murmured as he walked out of the door and out of her life, for good.

26

─────────

SIX WEEKS LATER

I t had been over a month since Hayden had seen or even heard from Austin. He hadn't sent her any funny emails or responded to her texts about her upcoming show in Compton Pass. She'd extended a blanket invite to him, his parents, aunts, uncles, cousins, or anyone else who wanted to come and had even reserved some tickets for them.

It didn't mean much since it was a small, rural venue, but she'd sold out a show for the very first time. When the club's entertainment manager had given her the good news, along with a bonus she never thought she'd earn, her gut reaction had been to run and tell Austin. Except she didn't think he cared anymore.

The stab in her guts following that realization eclipsed her excitement over meeting her next career goal. Which made her wonder if she might have had some of her priorities skewed.

Hayden was starting to wonder if her greatest mistake in her previous relationship had been sticking with a bad decision long after she realized she'd made one. Taking action to put her life back on track in a timely fashion, no matter how hard that might be, seemed like a better plan. It had been scary as fuck, but if she'd done it sooner she'd have been so much better off.

Well, shit. That was easier to see now that she'd gained some independence and started having some success. She might never be a superstar, but she knew she could support herself if she had to.

Hayden took her new cell phone out of her back pocket and opened the messaging app Austin used to chat with the rest of the Compass boys. No more relying on free library internet once or twice a day for her!

It only took a few clicks to find him. Before she could chicken out, she wrote, *Hey, not sure if you got my voicemail, but I'm playing a show in Compton Pass tonight. Would love to see you if you're in town and don't have anything better to do.*

Crickets. Digital fucking crickets.

Despite the green ring around his picture, which indicated he was active right then, Austin said nothing. Had fulfilling one of her dreams cost her another? If she could rewind a few months and only pick one, which one would she choose?

The pain Hayden hadn't suffered from in months came out of nowhere and exploded in her side. Or maybe that was what it felt like when her heart broke.

Hours later, Hayden couldn't say how she'd made it through her entire set list without breaking down during every sad song. But here she was, at the end of her show. Despite combing the crowd repeatedly during her performance, she hadn't seen a single familiar face.

None of the Comptons had come, not even Austin.

Hell, he probably hadn't even told his family she was in town. She regretted not reaching out to Leah or Hope or...well, any of them who might have put in a good word for her after the show, really. Even if they had been understandably reluctant to interfere, she would have loved to see them again.

Despite her place in the spotlight, surrounded by more

than a hundred people giving her their rapt attention, she felt utterly alone. Had she proven she was tough enough to make it on her own, or only that she hadn't been tough enough to make herself vulnerable again?

"I have one more song for you all tonight." And though she'd planned something entirely different for her finale, there was only one song on the tip of her tongue. "It's an acoustic version of a classic. One of my favorites. I hope you enjoy it. And if there's someone in your life you wish would stay there, make sure you let them know before it's too late."

She closed her eyes, took a deep breath, then performed her rearranged medley of Jackson Browne's "The Load-Out" and "Stay (Just A Little Bit Longer)." She'd toyed with it every single night since she'd gotten her campervan and Austin had walked away without even coming to look at it.

Hayden had never sung a song so close to her heart before. Everything receded but the music and the conduit to share her feelings with the world. Yes, she loved this moment—the high she got from performing. Every other instant of her day was empty without Austin to share it with.

By the time she got to the "Stay" portion of her arrangement, she realized how badly she'd screwed things up. It horrified her when her voice cracked, full of tears by the final notes she delivered.

When she put down her guitar, there was absolute silence. She wondered if she'd gone deaf for a heartbeat, until the crowd erupted into a cacophony of shouts, cheers, and claps.

Hayden blinked the world back into focus. And right there, dead center in the front row, was Austin. He leapt onstage and strode toward her.

"Did you mean that?" he asked.

She shrieked and flew to him, nearly bowling him over when she hopped so that she would wrap both her arms and legs around him. "You came."

"But I'm not sure if I should have." He swallowed so hard she heard it despite the whistles from the audience. Instead of hugging her tight, like he usually did, he barely patted her back. Hayden unwound herself from him and slipped to the ground so she could meet his serious stare. "So tell me, did you mean what you said and what you sang?"

"I did." She nodded.

That was all it took. Austin scooped her up and carried her from the bar.

He deposited her in the passenger seat of an older pick-up he'd obviously borrowed from the ranch then drove her away.

27

Austin shut off the truck's engine and lights. He knew that if he brought Hayden upstairs, the night was only going to end one way. They were going to make love because when they were together, they couldn't resist each other.

What would the new dawn bring?

He'd barely managed to keep from responding to her messages since the last time he swore he was done. Addicted to her, if he fell off the wagon tonight it was going to be nearly impossible to go cold turkey again.

It was the glimmer of hope her final song choice had sown in his heart that made it impossible for him not to persist. He bowed his head and thought about what his family would tell him to do. Jake's voice came into his mind. "You have to be patient with any animal, including a person, that's been wounded by another. It takes unbelievable courage to trust again. Be relentless in your kindness. Be forgiving and endless with your chances. Eventually you will be rewarded."

He thought about the man and how he'd lived his entire life without his soul mate. That much pain could never add up to the small hurt of Hayden leaving again if she chose to later on. He could always try again. Would always try again, because he believed they were meant to be together.

He got out of the truck and held the door open before gesturing for her to climb the stairs. "Come in, please?"

She nodded and took his hand as they ascended together.

Hayden crossed through the kitchen on the way to his bedroom. Neither of them bothered to pretend that wasn't where they were destined to end up. Her finger trailed along the oven as she passed it before looking up at the photograph of JD and Vicky. He thought he saw her nod, almost to herself. Or maybe to them. What was she thinking?

After months of disappointment and regret, he was afraid to believe her actions tonight could be signs of a lasting change in her philosophy. Pushing her now might drive her away forever.

So maybe he would learn to be happy with what she could give.

Seeing her here again, in his space, had every manly part of him standing at attention. The past month had shown him that something was definitely better than nothing. "God, Hayden, I missed you."

"I missed you, too." She looked over her shoulder and asked, "Unzip my dress?"

Fuck yes he would. Austin slid it down her back, admiring the creamy skin revealed and dotting it with kisses as he went. And when it dropped to the floor at her feet, he helped her step out of the flowy material, which left her standing before him in nude heels and the sexiest bra and panty set he'd ever seen. Wine-colored lace decorated her skin and gave him glimpses of the treasures beneath.

"Is that for me?"

"I was wishing you'd come." She trembled then. "I didn't think you would, but I hoped…"

"Shit, I'm sorry I cut you off like that." He rushed to her and kissed her because he couldn't stand not to for another moment.

"I hurt you." She frowned as she took another taste of his lips. "I didn't realize I had the power to do that."

"I think that's the problem here. All along you haven't seen what I've seen. You haven't known how strong you are. I do. It's one of the things I love best about you."

"Is the way it feels when you fuck me another thing you like best?" She bent over the bed and crawled onto it, flashing her ass, which was hardly obscured by her tiny thong. She'd been tempting before when she'd been kind of broken and timid. This side of her, the wildcat side, was utterly irresistible.

"Hell yes." Austin kicked off his boots, then tore at his shirt and pants as if they were the sort strippers used with Velcro along the seams.

He stalked to the bed and joined her. Tonight he wasn't holding anything back. She'd proved she was tough enough to handle him. All of him. So he planned to give her everything he had.

Austin grabbed her wrists and pinned them above her head with one of his hands. "Don't move."

"Or what?"

"I'll spank your ass until you're so damn hot you beg me to fuck you," he swore.

"Can't we skip all that if I beg you now? I need you, Austin." She spread her legs, tempting him to rush.

"No. Some things are meant to be savored." Besides, he had to make this the best sex of her life if there was any way he was going to convince her to stay this time.

Once he started making love to her, he got a little carried away. It might have been hours that he spent kissing her all over as his hands caressed and teased. He spent quality time suckling her breasts and fully appreciating the lingerie she'd bought and worn for him before he removed it.

Then he slithered down to slip her heels from her feet. He massaged them as he licked a path from her ankles back toward her core. And when he peeled her panties down her thighs and flung them somewhere in the corner of the room, he buried his face in her pussy.

Overwhelmed by her scent and taste, he feasted on her.

When he added his fingers to the mix, she arched from the bed.

"Not so fast." He withdrew, licking the digits clean. "Tonight I want you to wait for me. Come with me. I want us to be in this together."

"We are." She reached for his shoulders, as if to pull him into his place between her thighs.

Austin flipped her over so fast she squeaked, though out of excitement, not fear. She didn't cower from him. No, she got on her knees and shoved her ass in the air for him.

"That's better." He slapped her firm cheek lightly. Just enough to spike her arousal with a hint of pain.

"More," she pleaded as she rocked toward his palm. So he spanked her a few more times before blanketing her. When he mounted her, she moaned.

So did he.

This was where she belonged, in his bed and in his life. Not only for a night or two at a time, either.

They were made to be together. He was sure of it.

Austin bit her shoulder as he entered her, incapable of finesse. He hoped she understood that this was a claim. Not the sort that would bind her against her will, but a promise to be hers every bit as she was his.

When he'd buried himself balls-deep in her steaming pussy, he grabbed her hips and began to pump. He roared as he tossed his head back and prayed for stamina.

"I'm going to come, Austin." She groaned and quaked as he pounded into her.

"Not yet." He reached beneath her and pinched her nipple.

That really wasn't an effective tool for stalling her arousal. He only seemed to encourage it. She pushed back against him, increasing the pace and power of his thrusts.

Austin leaned forward and pressed his finger to her lips. She opened her mouth and sucked him as wildly as she'd devoured his cock when she'd gone down on him in his truck that day. The memory alone had him slipping toward the edge of rapture.

So he withdrew his now spit-slicked finger and returned it to her ass when he notched it against her asshole.

Hayden kicked her feet and shouted his name as he invaded her rear while riding her faster and harder. She hugged his cock and his hand, doing her best to keep them joined despite their wild pistoning.

And when her thighs gave out and she fell forward on the mattress, he knew it was time.

He used his free hand to wrap in her hair and turn her face to the side.

Then he followed her down so that as much of their bodies were connected as possible when he took her mouth in a searing kiss.

Austin paused only to shout, "Now, Hayden! Let go."

She spasmed on the bed beneath him, making it impossible for him to resist. He joined her in orgasm, sure his come was splashing into the deepest parts of her. He'd never felt so connected to someone as he did in that moment, and not because of his cock or his finger buried within her.

It was her eyes, which flew open and stared directly into his as she shattered, that grounded him. Another wave of his climax crashed over him while she watched. He continued to empty himself into her until she'd taken every last drop he had to give.

And only then did he reluctantly withdraw from her body.

He reached for his shirt to clean them up, then gathered her to his chest. They were silent for a while, exchanging periodic kisses, like the last bit of popcorn popping before it was done.

They floated back to earth together.

Eventually Hayden hummed and stretched, then cleared her throat. Austin braced himself for her farewell kiss. It would slash his soul to bits after what they'd just shared. He begged the universe to let him be strong enough to watch her go again if she chose to leave.

Because the truth was...he loved her. And if this was what it took for her to be happy, so be it.

Never did he expect what came out of her lush lips next.

28

———

"Austin?"

"Yeah, baby?" He took a huge breath then let it out with a wheeze that made her wonder if he'd fucked her well enough to injure himself. His abs clenched and his hands balled in the sheets. Hopefully what she was about to say would take his mind off any pain she'd unintentionally caused him.

"Do you think I could stay? Just a little bit longer?" She summoned every scrap of bravery she had and went all in. He was worth the risk. "Like...possibly forever?"

Her strong, gallant cowboy trucker sat up straight so fast, he nearly tumbled her off the edge of the bed. "Are you fucking serious?"

Ummm...had she read the situation wrong?

"I know we kid around about that *stay* thing, but it's not really a joke to me," Austin said. His hands flew out and steadied her before she fell, just like always.

Only this time his support didn't make her feel like a student driver whose instructor had just slammed on their emergency brake. It felt like a racecar driver wearing a five-point harness because it allowed them to go faster—perform better—without risking their lives.

Hayden couldn't wait to commit to him and give him a similar advantage.

"I'm not playing games with you." She scooted toward him and he took her cue, drawing her into his lap. "I've been thinking a lot about this. Us. I'm willing to admit I made a mistake by letting you go because while I proved to myself that I can survive, I never feel as alive and as complete as I do when I'm with you. That's more important than just existing."

"You'd give up your music for me?" He frowned. "While I'd like to be a selfish bastard about this, I don't think that's the right answer."

"I would if I had to, but I'm getting greedy now. I want my career *and* I want you. What about this?" She swallowed hard. "What if we plan out places you need to be at certain times of the year? Common roads you travel between here and the processing plants and your biggest customers."

Austin started to smile before she'd even finished. He jumped in, nodding, squeezing her kind of tight as they envisioned their future together, not that she was about to complain. "You can set up gigs along or near those routes."

"Plus I could play at open mic nights we come across or ask if I can perform for tips at places we stop at for the night in between bigger performances. We could travel together. Save on gas and carpool. Or truckpool. Whatever, you know what I mean."

He speared his fingers into her hair and cradled her head against his shoulder. "You really want that? To team up instead of taking on the world by yourself? I believe you're plenty capable of conquering anything you set your mind to. You've made it very apparent that you don't *need* me."

"I know. But I want you. Bad." She leaned in and raked her teeth over his stubbled jaw, staking her claim.

"I think I might have passed out after I came so damn hard. Am I dreaming?" He groaned. "I've been dying to hear you say these things for a while now."

"Forgive me, Austin." She stroked his cheek before leaning in to kiss him. "I had to figure it out on my own. I love you for letting me do that."

"You what?" His smile turned into a wicked grin as he revealed the patient predator she knew he was inside.

"I love you." She practiced saying it out loud. She had a feeling she'd be doing that a lot.

"Don't make any mistakes about this, Hayden." He stared into her eyes as he finished fusing their souls. "I love you, too. To the ends of the earth and back. Wherever you go, I will follow you."

"I'd rather you drive."

"Speaking of that..." He cleared his throat. "There's something I'd like to show you."

"I don't need to see it. I can feel it. And that's way better." Hayden rubbed up against him, shocked he could be getting hard again so soon. He'd completely undone her.

"Not that." A laugh burst from Austin's chest. "Well, okay. Yes, that. But something else first."

She tipped her head. "What?"

He turned around and showed her his naked back, which would never truly be bare again. It was entirely covered with ink.

"Austin, oh my God." She gasped and flew to him, touching his new artwork as if to see if it was a real tattoo and not some kind of illusion. "It's incredible. The portraits of Jake and your parents are insane. They look like photographs."

He didn't speak, letting her explore, wondering when she would see it.

Her fingertip traced the letters in the banner that flowed

above and below the scene, framing it. She read it out loud, "Heaven on Earth."

In between, below the faces of the foundational members of his family, was a long and winding road that originated from the ridge at Compton Ranch, which made a background for his rig. Inside it were two much smaller, though no less spectacular, portraits.

"Look, you're driving!" She squealed as she took in the details, which led her to the person at the center of it all. "Is that—?"

"It seemed appropriate. You are my favorite passenger, after all." He turned around then, in time to kiss away the happy tears that began to roll down her cheeks.

"What if I didn't reach out? What if..."

"I would have carried you with me wherever I went until you were ready for me. For this. For us," he promised.

It was the most glorious feeling in the world when she said it again. "I love you."

He knew now what had been strong enough to keep the couples in his family together. Until he'd experienced it himself, he hadn't fully understood the unbreakable bonds they'd forged or how they could last beyond a lifetime.

Austin couldn't wait to tell James, Bryant, and Doug what they were missing and hoped they'd find out for themselves someday soon.

Until then, he planned to do his part to keep the Compass legacy of love going strong. "I love you too, Hayden. I always will."

If you've enjoyed the Heaven on Earth, be sure to check out the continuing Compass saga in Into the Fire, Compass Boys Book Two, for James and Ivy's story.

Compass Boys, Book 2

A brand new, never before released standalone story in the Compass saga from New York Times and USA Today bestselling authors Jayne Rylon and Mari Carr.

James Compton is a man with his feet firmly planted in two different worlds. Six months out of the year, he's Seth's oldest boy, working with his family and the horses on Compass Ranch. The other half, he's Jamie, a daring smokejumper on the West Yellowstone Squad. Those two halves have always made him feel complete, happy, satisfied. Then he meets his boss's daughter, Ivy...

Ivy Wagner recognizes the irony that is her life. With her college degree in hand, she is ready to embark on her career as a large animal vet. Add to that, the attentiveness of a very sexy James Compton and her future should be all sunshine and steamy shared showers. However, a devastating loss in Ivy's past has ensured she will never date a smokejumper...no matter how perfect James is for her.

As James and Ivy grow closer, it's clear they're both headed toward a day of reckoning. Ivy can't lose anyone else she loves to the wild fires that rage and James isn't sure he's capable of giving up a vital part of himself, of living half a life.

When someone close to James dies, the pair are forced to face their demons and figure out what to let go and what to fight for.

Click here to buy Into the Fire.

If you haven't already read the rest of the Compass saga, be sure to go back and read all about the original Compass brothers (Silas, Seth, Sam, and Sawyer) and their daughters, the Compass Girls (Sienna, Hope, Jade, and Sterling). You'll enjoy their stories as much as Hayden did!

The adventure begins with Northern Exposure. Click here to find out more.

ABOUT THE AUTHORS

Jayne Rylon and Mari Carr met at a writing conference in June 2009 and instantly became arch enemies. Two authors couldn't be more opposite. Mari, when free of her librarian-by-day alter ego, enjoys a drink or two or... more. Jayne, allergic to alcohol, lost huge sections her financial-analyst mind to an epic explosion resulting from Mari gloating about her hatred of math. To top it off, they both had works in progress with similar titles and their heroes shared a name. One of them would have to go.

The battle between them for dominance was a bloody, but short one, when they realized they'd be better off combining their forces for good (or smut). With the ink dry on the peace treaty, they emerged as good friends, who have a remarkable amount in common despite their differences, and their writing partnership has flourished. Except for the time Mari attempted to poison Jayne with a bottle of Patron. Accident or retaliation? You decide.

Join Mari's newsletter and Jayne's Naughty News so you don't miss new releases, contests, or exclusive subscriber-only content.

Find Jayne Rylon on the web:
Twitter - @JayneRylon
Facebook - JayneRylon

www.jaynerylon.com

contact@jaynerylon.com

Find Mari Carr on the web at

www.maricarr.com

mari@maricarr.com

ALSO BY JAYNE RYLON

MEN IN BLUE

Hot Cops Save Women In Danger

Night is Darkest

Razor's Edge

Mistress's Master

Spread Your Wings

Wounded Hearts

Bound For You

DIVEMASTERS

Sexy SCUBA Instructors By Day, Doms On A Mega-Yacht By Night

Going Down

Going Deep

Going Hard

POWERTOOLS

Five Guys Who Get It On With Each Other & One Girl. Enough Said?

Kate's Crew

Morgan's Surprise

Kayla's Gift

Devon's Pair

Nailed to the Wall

Hammer it Home

HOT RODS

Powertools Spin Off. Keep up with the Crew plus...

Seven Guys & One Girl. Enough Said?

King Cobra

Mustang Sally

Super Nova

Rebel on the Run

Swinger Style

Barracuda's Heart

Touch of Amber

Long Time Coming

STANDALONE

Menage

Middleman

4-Ever Theirs

Nice & Naughty

Contemporary

Where There's Smoke

Report For Booty

COMPASS BROTHERS

Modern Western Family Drama Plus Lots Of Steamy Sex

Northern Exposure

Southern Comfort

Eastern Ambitions

Western Ties

COMPASS GIRLS

*Daughters Of The Compass Brothers Drive Their Dads Crazy And Fall
In Love*

Winter's Thaw

Hope Springs

Summer Fling

Falling Softly

COMPASS BOYS

Sons Of The Compass Brothers Fall In Love

Heaven on Earth

Into the Fire

Still Waters

Light as Air

PLAY DOCTOR

Naughty Sexual Psychology Experiments Anyone?

Dream Machine

Healing Touch

RED LIGHT

A Hooker Who Loves Her Job

Complete Red Light Series Boxset

FREE - Through My Window - FREE

Star

Can't Buy Love

Free For All

PICK YOUR PLEASURES

Choose Your Own Adventure Romances!

Pick Your Pleasure

Pick Your Pleasure 2

RACING FOR LOVE

MMF Menages With Race-Car Driver Heroes

Complete Series Boxset

Driven

Shifting Gears

PARANORMALS

Vampires, Witches, And A Man Trapped In A Painting

Paranormal Double Pack Boxset

Picture Perfect

Reborn

PENTHOUSE PLEASURES

Six Naughty Manhattanite Neighbors Find Kinky Love

Taboo

Kinky

Voyeur

Sinner

Mentor

Fetish

ALSO BY MARI CARR

<u>Wild Irish:</u>

Come Monday

Ruby Tuesday

Waiting for Wednesday

Sweet Thursday

Friday I'm in Love

Saturday Night Special

Any Given Sunday

Wild Irish Christmas

January Girl

<u>Compass:</u>

Northern Exposure

Southern Comfort

Eastern Ambitions

Western Ties

Winter's Thaw

Hope Springs

Summer Fling

Falling Softly

<u>**Farpoint Creek**</u>

Outback Princess

Outback Cowboy

Outback Master

Outback Lovers

<u>Bundles</u>

Cowboy Heat

What Women Want

Scoundrels

<u>Individual Titles:</u>

Sugar and Spice

Everything Nice

Erotic Research

Tequila Truth

Rough Cut

Happy Hour

Power Play

Slam Dunk

One Daring Night

Assume the Positions

Seducing the Boss

<u>Just Because:</u>

Because of You

Because You Love Me

Because It's True

<u>Second Chances:</u>

Fix You

Full Moon

Status Update

The Back-Up Plan

Never Been Kissed

Say Something

<u>Trinity Masters:</u>

Elemental Pleasure

Primal Passion

Scorching Desire

Forbidden Legacy

Hidden Devotion

Elegant Seduction

Secret Scandal

Delicate Ties

<u>Big Easy:</u>

Blank Canvas

Crash Point

Full Position

Rough Draft

Triple Beat

Winner Takes All

Going Too Fast

<u>Sparks in Texas:</u>

Sparks Fly

Waiting for You

Something Sparked

Off Limits

No Other Way

Whiskey Eyes

<u>Lowell High:</u>

Bound by the Past

Covert Affairs

Mad about Meg

<u>Madison Girls</u>

Kiss Me Kate

Three Reasons Why

<u>June Girls:</u>

No Recourse

No Regrets

<u>Boys of Fall:</u>

Free Agent

Red Zone

Wild Card

<u>Cocktales</u>

Party Naked

Screwdriver

Bachelor's Bait

Screaming O

WHAT WAS YOUR FAVORITE PART?

Did you enjoy this book? If so, please leave a review and tell your friends about it. Word of mouth and online reviews are immensely helpful and greatly appreciated.

JAYNE'S SHOP

Check out Jayne's online shop for autographed print books,
direct download ebooks, reading-themed apparel up to size
5XL, mugs, tote bags, notebooks, Mr. Rylon's wood (you'll have
to see it for yourself!) and more.
www.jaynerylon.com/shop

LISTEN UP!

The majority of Jayne's books are also available in audio format on Audible, Amazon and iTunes.

www.ingramcontent.com/pod-product-compliance
Lightning Source LLC
Chambersburg PA
CBHW071255190726
48292CB00007B/2551